Raul stilled, paralyzed with shock. *Dio!* It was impossible! But she felt so tight around him.

Heart pumping as if he had run a marathon, he drew back a fraction, stunned and uncomprehending when he saw that Libby was holding her knuckles against her mouth. Her eyes were dilated with shock. But she could not be a virgin. The idea was inconceivable.

CHANTELLE SHAW lives on the English coast, five minutes from the sea, and does much of her thinking about the characters in her books while walking on the beach. An avid reader from an early age, she found that school friends used to hide their books when she visited, but Chantelle would retreat into her own world, and she still writes stories in her head all the time. Chantelle has been blissfully married to her own tall, dark and very patient hero for more than twenty years and has six children. She began to read Harlequin® romances as a teenager, and throughout the years of being a stay-at-home mom to her brood, found romance fiction helped her to stay sane! Her aim is to write books that provide an element of escapism, fun and of course romance for the countless women who juggle work and a home life and who need their precious moments of "me" time. She enjoys reading and writing about strong-willed, feisty women and even stronger-willed sexy heroes. Chantelle is at her happiest when writing. She is particularly inspired while cooking dinner, which unfortunately results in a lot of culinary disasters! She also loves gardening, taking her very badly behaved terrier for walks and eating chocolate (followed by more walking—at least the dog is slim!).

UNTOUCHED UNTIL MARRIAGE

CHANTELLE SHAW

~ WEDLOCKED! ~

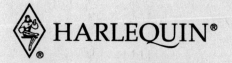

TORONTO • NEW YORK • LONDON
AMSTERDAM • PARIS • SYDNEY • HAMBURG
STOCKHOLM • ATHENS • TOKYO • MILAN • MADRID
PRAGUE • WARSAW • BUDAPEST • AUCKLAND

Recycling programs
for this product may
not exist in your area.

ISBN-13: 978-0-373-88172-7

UNTOUCHED UNTIL MARRIAGE

First North American Publication 2011

Copyright © 2010 by Chantelle Shaw

UNTOUCHED UNTIL MARRIAGE

CHAPTER ONE

ACCORDING to the private investigator he had hired, he would find his father's mistress here. Raul Carducci stepped out of his limousine and glanced along the quayside of the Cornish fishing village. Nature's Way—Health Foods and Herbal Remedies sat between an ice-cream parlour and a gift shop, both of which were shut and, from their abandoned air, would not open again until the start of the summer season.

Drizzle fell relentlessly from the leaden sky and he grimaced as he turned up his coat collar. The sooner he could return to Italy, where the spring sunshine was already warming the sparkling blue waters of Lake Bracciano, the better, he thought grimly. But he had come to Pennmar to follow the instructions set out in Pietro Carducci's will, and without further pause he strode towards the one shop in the parade that was open for custom.

* * *

Libby was so engrossed in studying the end-of-year financial report for Nature's Way that it took a few seconds for the sound of the windchimes which hung above the shop door to impinge on her brain. The chimes had not been a regular sound throughout the winter, she acknowledged ruefully as she lifted her eyes from the column of red figures in the accounts book. Customers had been few and far between after visitors to Pennmar had returned home at the end of the previous summer, and now the business was on the verge of bankruptcy.

Opening a health food shop in a remote Cornish village had been another of her mother's hare-brained schemes, Libby thought ruefully. The small inheritance from Libby's grandmother had quickly been swallowed up in refurbishing the shop, but her mother, with typical blind optimism, had been certain the business would be a success.

Thinking about Liz caused the familiar dull ache in Libby's chest, but a customer was waiting to be served, and she hurriedly pushed aside the beaded curtain that separated the back office from the shop. The man had his back to her, so that she was faced with formidably broad shoulders cloaked in a pale suede car coat. He was prowling restlessly around the shop, so tall that his head brushed against the roof beams, and Libby sensed the inherent strength of his big, powerful body.

'Can I help you?' she began brightly, but her smile faltered when the stranger swung round and trapped her with his piercing dark stare. He was not your average tourist, she realised. Indeed, there was nothing remotely average about this man. Hair as sleek and dark as a raven's wing was swept back from his brow. His chiselled features, razor-sharp cheekbones and a square chin were softened slightly by the sensual curve of his mouth, and his olive-gold skin gleamed like satin beneath the bright shop light. He was, beyond doubt, the most stunningly handsome man Libby had ever seen. She could not tear her gaze from him, and blushed when his eyes narrowed speculatively on her face.

Raul trailed his eyes over the shop-girl's purple patterned skirt and acid green top and shuddered. Bohemian chic might have featured on the Paris catwalks recently, but he preferred women to look elegant and groomed in haute couture. The tie-dyed hippy look did nothing for him.

But she was startlingly pretty, he conceded as he studied her oval face with its high cheekbones, surrounded by a mane of bright red curls that tumbled halfway down her back. Her vivid hair contrasted with her alabaster complexion, and even from a distance of a few feet away he could see the sprinkling of golden freckles across her nose and cheeks. Eyes the deep blue-green of the sea on a stormy day surveyed him from beneath long gold lashes, and from somewhere the unbidden idea slid into his head that her soft pink lips were infinitely kissable.

Frowning at this unwelcome train of thought, he lowered his gaze and winced at her lime-green tights and purple boots before his eyes were drawn back to her face. Her mouth was a fraction too wide, but that only seemed to enhance her appeal. Dressed in a designer gown rather than her garish outfit she would be exceptionally beautiful, Raul acknowledged, irritated by the unexpected tug of sexual interest that coiled in his gut.

His jaw tightened. His business was with his father's mistress, not this girl, and he suppressed the inappropriate urge to cover her lush mouth with his lips. 'I'm looking for Elizabeth Maynard,' he said abruptly.

The man's voice was deep-timbred, as rich and sensual as molten chocolate, and his pronounced accent was innately sexy. Italian, Libby hazarded a guess as she studied his golden skin and obsidian eyes. It was not every day that a drop-dead sexy man walked into the shop. He was, in fact, the only person to have entered Nature's Way all morning, she thought ruefully. Good manners dictated that she should answer him, but she had had an unconventional childhood, where hiding from loan sharks or speaking through the letterbox to the bailiffs while her mother escaped out of the bathroom window had been a frequent occurrence, and she was instinctively wary of strangers.

Another thought slipped into her head that caused her stomach to tie itself in a knot. True, the man did not look like a social worker—and she'd met plenty of those as a child—but what if he was here about Gino?

'Who are you?' she asked sharply.

Raul frowned. He had spent most of his life surrounded by servants whose sole duty was to please him and jump to his bidding without question. He saw no reason why he should explain himself to a shop-girl, and his eyes narrowed as he fought to control his impatience. 'My name is Raul Carducci.'

The girl drew a sharp breath and her eyes widened until they seemed to dominate her face. 'Pietro Carducci's son?' she faltered.

Raul stiffened with outrage. Had his father's

mistress discussed the Carducci family with her staff? he wondered furiously. Had she boasted of her affair with a rich Italian aristocrat to the whole damned village? He glared at the curtained doorway, trying to see if the owner of the shop was lurking behind it, but his view was obscured by the strings of gaudy plastic beads.

He gave an impatient shrug. '*Si*, Pietro Carducci was my father. But my business is with Ms Maynard—so if you would please inform her that I am here.' He could no longer contain the bitterness that had eaten away at him like a corrosive poison since he had been informed of the terms of his father's will, and he bit out savagely, 'No doubt she will be delighted when she learns that giving birth to my father's illegitimate son has ensured her a meal-ticket for life. She will no longer have to scrape a living from running *this* place,' he added, casting a disparaging glance at the array of health foods and potions, the stacks of decorative candles, and the smouldering joss-sticks that gave off a peculiar sickly scent as they burned. 'I fear, *signorina*, that you will soon have to look for another job.'

Libby stared at Raul Carducci in dumbstruck silence. Her mother had mentioned that Pietro had a son, but Liz's affair with her Italian lover had been no more than a brief holiday fling, and she had learned few details about his family. Her mum hadn't even realised that Pietro was the head of the world-famous Carducci Cosmetics company until she'd read an article in a magazine about him while she'd been waiting for an antenatal appointment, Libby thought bitterly. Liz had agonised over whether to tell her lover she was pregnant, but when she had finally written to him to inform him she had given birth to his child Pietro had not bothered to reply.

But although Pietro Carducci had not acknowledged his child, he must have told his older son about Gino, Libby realised shakily. Raul's harsh words, *my father's illegitimate son*, filled her with a deep sense of unease. He sounded far from delighted about the existence of his half-brother. She did not know what to say, and while she hesitated the silence was broken by the jangling sound of the windchimes above the door.

Raul glanced round to see a woman manoeuvre a pushchair into the shop. 'Here we are, Gino, back in the warm,' the woman said cheerfully, her voice barely audible over the yells coming from beneath the buggy hood. She lifted the waterproof plastic cover,

revealing the screwed up face of a screaming baby boy. 'All right, my lovely. I'll get
you out in a second.'

Raul's eyes were drawn to the pushchair,
and some indefinable emotion gripped him
as he focused on the baby's olive skin and
tight black curls. The woman had called the
child Gino, and even though he was less than
a year old there could be no mistaking his
resemblance to his father. *Dio!* Raul thought
numbly. He had been determined to demand
a DNA test to prove the child's paternity,
but there was no need. Indisputably this was
Pietro Carducci's son.

He turned his attention to the woman,
noting her ruddy cheeks, coarse brown hair
and the lumpy figure shrouded in a beige
coat. It seemed astounding that Pietro, whose
love of classical beauty had led him to build
a priceless art collection, had chosen this
dowdy woman as his mistress—and it was
even more impossible to imagine the woman
working in a lap-dancing club!

Raul's mouth tightened as he recalled his
meeting eight months ago with the lawyer his
father had appointed as executor of his will.

'"This is the last will and testament of
Pietro Gregorio Carducci,' Signor Orsini
had read aloud. '"It is my wish that control

of my company, Carducci Cosmetics, be shared equally between my adopted son, Raul Carducci, and my infant son and only blood heir Gino Maynard."'

Seeing that Raul had been struck dumb by the revelation that Pietro had a secret child, the lawyer had continued reading. "'I leave to my two sons, Raul and Gino, equal share of the Villa Giulietta. It is my wish that Gino should grow up in the family home. His share of the company and the villa are to be held in trust for him until he is eighteen, and until he is of age it is my wish that his mother, Elizabeth Maynard, will live at the villa with him, and will have control of Gino's share of CC."'

At that point Raul had sworn savagely, shocked beyond words at the news that he would not have sole control of the company he had been groomed for most of his life to run. He had found the expression 'blood heir' deeply wounding. He had been seven years old when Pietro and Eleonora Carducci had collected him from an orphanage in Naples and taken him to live at the Villa Giulietta. Pietro had always insisted that his adopted son was his rightful heir, who would one day inherit Carducci Cosmetics. Father and son had been close, and the bond between them had deepened after Eleonora's death ten years ago.

That was why it was so utterly unbelievable that Pietro had had a secret life, Raul thought bitterly. The man he had called Papa, the man he had wept for at Pietro's funeral, was suddenly a stranger who had deliberately withheld the fact that he had a mistress and a baby son.

'There is a clause in your father's will that I think you will find interesting,' Signor Orsini had murmured. 'Pietro has stated that if Ms Maynard should marry before Gino is eighteen, control of the child's share of CC would pass to you until he is of age. I imagine Pietro made this stipulation to protect the company should Ms Maynard make an unsuitable marriage,' the lawyer had added.

'Carducci Cosmetics will need all the protection it can get if I am forced to share the running of it with a lap-dancer,' Raul had growled savagely. 'My father must have been out of his mind.'

At that, Bernardo Orsini had shaken his head. 'Despite the fact that Pietro had been diagnosed with an aggressive brain tumour, I am absolutely certain that he was of sound mind when he made his will. His main concern was for his infant son.'

Raul dragged his mind back to the present and stared at the woman who had entered the shop. According to the lawyer, Elizabeth Maynard had worked as a lap-dancer at a club called the Purple Pussy Cat, but six months ago she had disappeared from her South London flat, owing her landlord several thousand pounds in rent arrears. Raul had visualised his father's mistress as a bleached blonde tart, but even though the drab woman who was lifting the baby out of the pushchair looked nothing like he had imagined, he still balked at the idea of her moving into the Villa Guilietta, while the prospect of sharing control of Carducci Cosmetics with her would be frankly amusing if he had not been consumed by rage and resentment at his father's dying wishes.

'I knew he'd stop crying the minute he saw his mummy,' the woman said cheerfully, and handed the child over to the young shop assistant.

Shock ricocheted through Raul. He stared—at first uncomprehendingly, and then with a growing sense of rage—as the flame-haired girl kissed away the tears from the baby's cheeks and settled him comfortably on her hip. His brain finally accepted what his eyes had seen.

'*You* are Elizabeth Maynard?' he demanded harshly.

The girl lifted her head and met his gaze. 'I am—although most people call me Libby.'

Raul did not give a damn what most people called her. He was still struggling to comprehend that this stunningly pretty girl had been his father's mistress. She could not be more than in her early twenties, and Pietro had been in his mid-sixties. Revulsion swept through him, and with it another emotion that filled him with self-disgust when he recognised it as jealousy. *Dio!* No wonder his father had kept quiet about this flame-haired siren. He had no problem picturing *her* working in a lap-dancing club, Raul thought as his eyes focused on the rounded contours of her breasts outlined beneath her stretchy top. An image flashed in his mind of her dancing in a skimpy costume, tossing her mane of fiery hair over her shoulders as she unfastened her bra and slowly let it drop…

He bit back an oath, infuriated by his body's involuntary reaction to his wayward thoughts. '*You* are Gino's mother?' He sought clarification, aware that he had initially jumped to the conclusion that the older woman had been his father's lover.

Libby hesitated. Margaret was making a

show of hunting through her handbag for something, but she was conscious of the older woman's avid curiosity. Her neighbour was a kindly woman, who often babysat Gino, but Margaret was an inveterate gossip. If she overheard that Libby was not Gino's mother, as everyone in Pennmar believed, but his sister, the news would be all around the village within the hour.

She recalled those first few terrible days after her mum had died. They had been living in London, packing for the move to Cornwall and the new life they had planned, when Liz had collapsed and never regained consciousness. Gino had only been three months old, and Libby had struggled to cope with her shock and grief while caring for her orphaned baby brother. Her friend Alice, a trainee lawyer, had been an invaluable help, but she had also warned Libby of the potential problems caused by Liz's death.

'If your mum didn't make a will and appoint you as Gino's guardian, then technically he becomes the responsibility of the State, and Social Services will decide who should care for him,' Alice had explained. 'Just because you are Gino's half-sister it doesn't mean they will automatically choose you.'

'But I've helped to care for him since the

day he was born,' Libby had argued, 'especially when Mum was so tired after his birth.'

Liz's long labour had left her exhausted. At the busy hospital where Gino had been born no one had mentioned the potential dangers of deep vein thrombosis, and when Liz had felt unusually breathless Libby had been unaware that it was a sign her mother had developed a blood clot which had lodged in one of her lungs.

Liz had died before the ambulance had arrived. There had been no time for mother and daughter to say goodbye, no chance for Liz to stipulate who should care for Gino, but Libby was utterly determined to bring up her baby brother and love him as her mother would have done. She had moved to Pennmar a week after Liz's funeral, to the shop they had set up with the money left by Libby's grandmother. Everyone in the village assumed that Gino was her baby. After Alice's warning that Social Services might take him from her, Libby had encouraged that misapprehension, and now she was reluctant to reveal the truth in front of Margaret.

She would explain the situation to Raul Carducci later, she decided, her sense of unease intensifying when she glanced at his hard face and saw no glimmer of warmth in his dark eyes. 'Yes, I'm Gino's mother,' she said quietly, a shiver running down her spine when his expression changed from cool disdain to savage contempt.

He flicked his eyes over her, and Libby felt acutely conscious that she had bought her top in a charity shop and had made her skirt from an old curtain. 'You are much younger than I had expected,' he said bluntly. He paused and then drawled softly, 'I'm curious to know what first attracted you to my sixty-five-year old billionaire father, Ms Maynard?'

His inference was plain. Raul thought she was a gold-digger who had had an affair with a wealthy older man for his money, Libby realised, colour storming into her cheeks. But she could not defend herself when Margaret had given up all pretence of searching in her handbag and was unashamedly listening to the conversation. Raul Carducci was an arrogant jerk, she thought angrily, her hot temper instantly flaring. 'Forgive me, but I don't think my relationship with your father is any of your business,' she told him tightly, her eyes flashing fire.

She could sense that Margaret was practically bursting with curiosity, and she forced a casual smile as she turned to the older woman.

'Thanks for taking Gino out. The doctor says that the sea air will help his chest.'

'You know I'll have him any time.' Margaret paused and glanced from Libby to her foreign-looking visitor. 'I could stay and mind him now, if you and the gentleman have things to discuss?'

Yes, and Margaret would waste no time sharing what she'd overheard with the rest of the village, Libby thought dryly. 'Thanks, but I must give Gino his lunch, and I don't want to take up any more of your time,' she said brightly. 'Could you put the '"Closed" sign on the door on your way out?'

Libby contained her impatience while a disgruntled looking Margaret ambled out of the shop, but the moment the older woman had shut the door she glared at Raul. 'I assume there is a reason for your visit, Mr Carducci, and you are not here merely to make disgusting innuendos?'

The unfamiliar sharpness of her voice unsettled Gino. He gave her a startled look and his lower lip trembled. Libby joggled him on her hip and patted his back, still furious with the man who was looking down his arrogant nose at her as if she were something unpleasant on the bottom of his shoe.

'Before you say anything else, I'd better

explain—' She broke off as Gino let out a wail and began to squirm in her arms. At ten months old he was surprisingly strong, and she struggled to hold him, dismay filling her when his cries turned into the familiar hacking cough that shook his frame. Immediately Libby's attention was focused exclusively on the baby, and she glanced distractedly at Raul. 'I must get him a drink. Excuse me,' she muttered, and hurried through the beaded curtain into the back part of the shop.

She took a beaker of juice the fridge, but Gino was crying and coughing too much for him to be able to drink. He was still wearing his thick outdoor suit, and his face was turning steadily redder as he overheated. Frantically Libby tried to unzip the suit with one hand and hold a hysterical, wriggling Gino in the other, conscious that Raul had followed her into the room and was watching her efforts.

'Here—let me hold him while you undress him,' he said abruptly, stepping forward and lifting the baby out of her arms before she could protest.

Gino was so startled that his cries subsided, but he was going through a particularly clingy stage at the moment and disliked strangers. Libby quickly tugged down the zip of his suit, waiting for him to renew his yells, but to her amazement he gave a little snuffle and stared fixedly at Raul's face.

'You must have a magic touch. Normally he screams blue murder if someone he doesn't know tries to hold him,' she muttered, feeling faintly chagrined as she freed Gino from the suit and he did not even glance at her. 'But Gino is a Gemini, and people born under that star sign are often very intuitive,' she added earnestly. 'Perhaps he instinctively recognises that there is a connection between the two of you. You are his brother—well, half-brother,' she amended, when Raul's dark brows rose sardonically.

'There is no blood link between us,' he informed her dismissively. 'Pietro was my adoptive father.' He saw the flash of surprise in Libby's eyes and wondered why he had felt the need to reveal that he had no bio-logical link to the father of her child. The idea that she and Pietro had shared a bed... He snapped a door shut on that particular image, infuriated that his eyes seemed to have a magnetic attraction to her breasts.

Elizabeth Maynard had been his father's mistress and had borne him a child; it was in-conceivable that he could be attracted to her. He forced his gaze up from her lush curves, moulded so enticingly beneath her clingy top, and stared at her face, his body stirring as he focused on the perfect cupid's bow of her mouth. Irritation with himself made his voice terse as he said abruptly, 'It's more likely the child was crying because he was scared you might drop him.'

'Of course I wasn't going to drop him,' Libby snapped furiously. She snatched Gino back into her arms and held the beaker of juice to his lips, frowning when she heard the horrible rasping sound in his chest as he breathed. 'I need to take him upstairs and give him his next dose of antibiotic,' she said edgily.

She glared at Raul who was leaning against her desk, unashamedly reading the financial report for Nature's Way. He dominated the small room, tall, dark and so disturbingly sexy that looking at him made her heart race uncomfortably fast. She hated the way he unsettled her and she wanted him to leave.

She crossed the room and slammed the accounts book shut. 'Why are you here?' she demanded bluntly. 'I read in the papers that Pietro had died. But that was more than six months ago, and in all that time no one from the Carducci family has ever been in contact.'

Raul gave her a look of haughty disdain. 'That is hardly my fault. You did a runner from your last address without paying the rent, and it has taken this long to find you. I am not here through choice, I assure you, Ms Maynard,' he told her scathingly. 'But my father stipulated in his will that he wanted his son to be brought up at the family home in Lazio—and so I have come to take Gino to Italy.'

CHAPTER TWO

For a few seconds Libby was too stunned to speak. Her friend Alice's warning reverberated in her head. 'Your mother didn't appoint you as Gino's guardian, and although you are his half-sister, legally you have no rights regarding his upbringing.'

If Liz had known she was going to die, of *course* she would have appointed her daughter as Gino's guardian, Libby thought desperately. But, as Alice had pointed out, she had no proof of her mother's wishes. It was ironic that Pietro Carducci, who had not even acknowledged his son's birth, should have made provision for Gino in his will. If the matter went to court, it seemed likely that Pietro's wishes would be taken into account, and possible that Raul would be granted custody of Gino and be allowed to take him to Italy.

Her heart was pounding with panic but one crucial thought stood out in Libby's

mind. Raul believed that Gino was *her* baby.
Clearly he had no idea that there had been
two Elizabeth Maynards, or that the woman
who had conceived Pietro Carducci's child as
a result of their brief affair had died only a
month after Pietro had passed away. She recalled the expression of disgust on Raul's face
when he had asked her what had attracted
her to his older, wealthy father. He believed
she was a gold-digger, but it was better he
thought that than discovered that she was
Gino's half-sister and had no legal claim on
him, she thought wildly.

She frowned, suddenly remembering something Raul had said. 'Why did you accuse me
of owing rent on the flat where we—I,' she
hastily amended, knowing she must hide the
fact that she had lived in London with her
mother, 'lived before I moved to Cornwall?
Of course I paid the rent.'

Raul's eyes narrowed at Libby's belliger-
ent tone. He was not used to being spoken
to in that manner by anyone, and certainly
not by a woman. His staff, both at the Villa
Giulietta and at Carducci Cosmetics, treated
him with the utmost respect, and the women
he mixed with socially tended to hang on
his every word. To his mind, a woman's role
was to make light conversation, to provide

soothing company after a day of hard bargaining in the boardroom and to grace his bed so that he could enjoy mutually satisfying sex without the complications of emotional involvement.

Elizabeth Maynard—or Libby, as she called herself, would be a far from soothing companion, he thought as he stared at her mass of wild red curls and stormy eyes. Her mouth was set in an angry line that challenged him to kiss her until her lips softened and parted and allowed him to slide his tongue between them. He inhaled sharply, and it took all of his formidable will-power to ignore the dictates of his body and listen to the cool logic of his brain. She was Pietro's tart, who had had no compunction about seducing a much older man with her nubile young body, and no way was the son going to repeat the mistakes of his father, Raul assured himself grimly.

'Your landlord said that you were frequently behind with the rent, and when you moved away suddenly you left owing him several thousand pounds,' he said coldly. 'Why would he lie?'

'To get back at me because I refused to sleep with him, most likely,' Libby muttered bitterly. 'He was a horrible old man. I used to take him the rent money regularly every month and he never missed an opportunity to try and grope me. He made it clear that he would reduce the rent if I "paid" him in another way.'

'Are you saying you weren't tempted?' Raul queried derisively. 'I assume you make a habit of sleeping with older men for financial gain. You certainly struck gold with my father,' he continued, ignoring her furious gasp. 'Having his child was a clever move, which I guess you thought would ensure you a meal ticket for life. You thought right; it has,' he said contemptuously. 'Pietro has granted you the right to bring up your son at the Carducci family villa, and take control of fifty percent of Carducci Cosmetics until Gino is eighteen.'

Raul gave a harsh laugh when Libby stared at him open-mouthed. He reached inside his coat and retrieved a sheaf of papers. 'Congratulations. You've hit the jackpot,' he drawled sarcastically as he thrust the documents at Libby.

She stared dazedly at the first page and saw that it was headed 'The last will and testament of Pietro Gregorio Carducci.' Conscious that Raul was watching her, she ran her eyes down the page until she came to a paragraph which stated that Gino's mother, Elizabeth

Maynard, should live at the Villa Giulietta, with all her expenses and living costs paid for out of the estate, until her son came of age.

It was astounding. She could barely comprehend it. But before she could read any further Gino made a grab for the documents. He was clearly fascinated by the white paper, and, remembering how he had shredded an important letter from the bank the previous day, Libby hastily handed the will back to Raul.

'So you mean you want me to live in Italy with Gino?' she said slowly, relief flooding through her that Raul hadn't sought her out to take the baby away from her. Not that she would have allowed him to, she thought fiercely. Gino was the only person she had left in the world, and she was prepared to do anything to keep him—even if that meant pretending that he was her son.

'I can't think of anything I'd like less,' Raul said, in a coldly arrogant tone that made her feel about two feet high. 'But unfortunately I have no say in the matter. My father clearly stated his wish that Gino and his mother should live at the Villa Giulietta.'

Libby glanced at her baby brother and felt her heart melt when he stared solemnly back at her with his big brown eyes. His light olive skin and mass of dark curls spoke of his Italian heritage, but he had her mother's smile, she thought, swallowing the sudden lump in her throat. Liz had adored her baby for the few short months she had spent with him. It seemed so desperately cruel that Gino had been robbed of his mother before he'd ever had a chance to know her, but she would take Liz's place, Libby vowed silently. Her little brother was her only link with her mum. She loved him just as deeply as if he was her own child, and she was determined to do what was best for him.

But would taking him to live in Italy, with Raul, who clearly resented his half-brother, really be in Gino's best interest? she brooded. Her doubts increased when she glanced at the autocratic features of the handsome Italian. 'We have things to talk about,' she said hesitantly. 'Perhaps we could meet in a day or two…'

Raul frowned impatiently. 'I don't have a day or two to waste hanging around here. And anyway, what is there to discuss? My father named Gino as his heir, and I can't believe you would turn down the chance to get your hands on his inheritance. Presumably you deliberately fell pregnant in the first place so that you could demand a massive payout in child maintenance?'

'I did no such thing,' Libby retorted angrily. Although he did not know it, Raul was insulting her mother, not her, and if she hadn't been holding Gino she would have slapped that arrogant smirk off his face. Far from deliberately falling pregnant, Liz had been utterly shocked when she had discovered that she had conceived a baby as a result of her holiday romance with a charming Italian.

'Gino was unplanned, it's true, but he was very wanted,' she told Raul huskily, remembering how Liz's shock had turned to delight that she was going to be a mother again. 'My mo—' She stopped in her tracks and continued hurriedly, 'Your father was informed of Gino's birth, but he never acknowledged his son and I never expected anything from him.'

Raul gave a disbelieving snort. 'My father was an honourable man who would never have turned his back on his child.' He frowned as a thought occurred to him. 'When was Gino born?'

'The seventh of June. He's ten months old now.'

'Pietro was very ill by June of last year, and he died in August,' Raul told her flatly. 'An inoperable brain tumour had been diagnosed the previous October and it grew rapidly. Did you know about his illness?' he asked Libby sharply.

She shook her head. Pietro must have fallen ill soon after her mother had returned from the Mediterranean cruise she had won. The cruise on which Liz had fallen in love with a gorgeous Italian, she had confessed to Libby, with a faintly embarrassed smile after all she had said over the years about the unreliability of men and the foolishness of losing your heart to one.

Liz had been devastated when she had heard nothing more from Pietro after the cruise—especially when she'd discovered that she had conceived his child. 'I've done it again, Libby,' she'd said tearfully, when she had emerged from the bathroom clutching a pregnancy test. 'I trusted a man and now I'm left with his baby—the same as happened with your bloody father. You'd think I'd have learned that all men are selfish bastards, wouldn't you?'

Libby had hated Pietro for hurting her mum, but according to Raul his father had returned to Italy from the cruise to learn that he was terminally ill. Perhaps he hadn't felt able to confide such devastating news to Liz, she thought, her heart aching for her mother and the man she had loved. When Liz had written to her lover to tell him of Gino's birth Pietro had been weeks from death, and maybe hadn't had the strength to reply. But surely the fact that he had included Liz and Gino in his will meant that he had cared for her mum after all?

Gino had been sitting quietly in her arms, but now he began to cough again, his chest heaving with the effort. 'I thought you said he was due some medication?' Raul commented, his frown deepening. He had as much experience of children as he had with aliens from another planet, but this baby sounded seriously unwell.

'He is.' Concern for Gino overrode Libby's reluctance to invite Raul up to the flat. 'You'd better come up,' she muttered.

'What's wrong with him?' Raul demanded when they reached the first floor landing.

Libby paused with her hand on the living room door. 'He had an illness called bronchiolitis, which is fairly common in babies, but he developed pneumonia and was very unwell. He was in hospital for a few weeks and now he can't seem to shake off this cough. The doctor said that the living conditions here don't help,' she confessed, recalling how the GP in the village had warned her that the mildew growing on the damp walls of the flat produced spores which Gino inhaled and were the worst thing for his lungs.

She pushed open the door, and stifled a groan at the scene of chaos that met her. Raul Carducci's unexpected visit had made her forget the disaster that had occurred the previous evening, when the bulge in her bedroom ceiling had given way and rain water had gushed through. Luckily, her friend Tony had been there. They had been sharing a bottle of wine while Libby had talked over her financial worries and the likelihood that she would have to close Nature's Way, and together they had grabbed her belongings and carried them into the sitting room, out of the deluge that had flooded her room. Tony had managed to block the hole to stop any more water pouring through, but he'd got soaked to the skin and had had to change into the sports gear that he kept in his car.

Her canvases were stacked against the sofa and her clothes heaped on the floor. Her underwear was on top of the pile, Libby noticed, flushing with embarrassment when she saw Raul's eyes rest on the numerous pairs of brightly coloured knickers. He glanced slowly around the room and she knew he was taking in the peeling wallpaper and the blue mould which had appeared on the wall again, despite the fact that she constantly scrubbed the area with fungal remover.

There had been so sign of damp when she and Liz had viewed the shop and flat the previous spring. Then, the place had seemed bright and airy, newly decorated, and with the windows flung open to allow the sea breeze to drift in. It was only during the wet winter that Libby had realised the rooms had been wallpapered to hide the patches of mildew.

She was irritated by the expression of distaste on Raul's face. It was clear from the superb quality of his clothes that he was very wealthy, and no doubt his home in Italy was a palace compared to the flat, but it was all she could afford—and actually even that was doubtful, she realised dismally when she remembered the letter from the bank that had informed her they would not increase her overdraft.

'Sorry about the mess,' she muttered. 'My bedroom was flooded last night and we piled all my things in here.'

'We?' Raul looked pointedly at the baby in Libby's arms.

'My friend Tony was here.' She followed Raul's gaze to the three empty wine bottles and two glasses on the coffee table, and watched his expression change from distaste to disapproval.

'Looks like you had quite a party,' he drawled.

Surely he didn't think they had got through three bottles of wine in one evening? 'Tony works in a bar and he brings me old wine bottles. I decorate them with decoupage and sell them at craft markets,' she explained. 'I'm an artist, and so is Tony,' she added, when Raul said nothing, just studied her with cool disdain in his eyes. Rebellion flared inside her. Why on earth did she feel she had to explain herself to this arrogant stranger?

Gino was wriggling to be set down. Libby's arms felt as though they were about to drop off from holding him and, distracted by Raul's brooding presence, she lowered the baby onto the floor and hurried into the tiny adjoining kitchen to fetch his medicine.

Gino immediately crawled over to the coffee table and reached towards one of the wine bottles. Raul grabbed him seconds before he pulled the glass bottle down on his head. The flat was a death-trap, he thought disgustedly as he swept the baby into his arms and stepped over the piles of junk on the floor to stand by the window. And there was an unpleasant musty smell in the room—caused, he guessed, by the fungus that was sprouting on the walls.

What was Elizabeth Maynard thinking of, bringing up her son in such appalling conditions? A pair of men's jeans was hanging over a chair, and he wondered if they belonged to the barman-cum-artist Tony, who had been here the previous night. Was he her lover? And, if so, what role did he have in Gino's life? Was he a stepfather to the child, or did Gino have a variety of 'uncles'?

Raul frowned, deeply disturbed by the idea. He knew what kind of woman Libby was: a lap-dancer and apparently an artist—or perhaps she meant *artiste*, he mused derisively. One thing was for sure. The sort of men who frequented strip-clubs were not likely to be suitable father figures for her baby. He pushed away the thought that his father had presumably met Libby at a club. He didn't want to think of Pietro like that. It sullied his memory. But, like it or not, his father had had an affair with Libby and she had borne him a child.

He looked down at Gino and was once more startled by the strong resemblance the baby had to Pietro. Gino's hair was a mass of tight curls, as his father's had been, and his big brown eyes had the same amber flecks. Pietro would have adored his baby son, Raul acknowledged. But Pietro had been dying when Gino had been born, and he had never seen his child. Raul could not understand why Pietro had not confided in him. All he could think was that his father had been ashamed of his relationship with a lap-dancer who was forty years younger than him. Perhaps he had suspected that Libby was a gold-digger, and that was why, in an effort to protect Gino, Pietro had stipulated that his infant son must spend his childhood at the Carducci family home.

It was a pity Pietro had included the child's mother in his will, Raul thought darkly. Libby clearly didn't have a clue about how to care for a baby. Gino had been staring out of the window, but he suddenly turned his head and gave Raul a gummy smile that revealed two little white teeth. The baby was cute, no doubt about that, Raul conceded. His mouth curved into an answering smile and he felt a sudden overwhelming feeling of protectiveness for Pietro's son. In that moment he knew that he wanted to care for Gino, and would love him—just as Pietro had cared for and loved *him*. This was his chance to repay his adoptive father for everything he had done for him. Pietro had made financial provision for his baby, but *he* would be a father figure to Gino, Raul vowed, and he was determined to make a damn sight better job of parenting than the boy's mother!

Libby hurried back from the kitchen. 'Would you mind holding him while I give him his medicine? He's not keen on it,' she added ruefully, thinking of the tussles she'd had, trying to persuade Gino to swallow the antibiotic.

She shook the bottle, poured the thick liquid into a spoon—and suddenly realised that in order to tip the medicine into Gino's mouth she would have to lean close to Raul. She tensed with the effort of trying not to touch him, but it was impossible to avoid him. Her senses flared, and she was conscious of the warmth emanating from his big body, the tactile softness of his suede coat and the drift of sandalwood cologne mingled with the fresh, clean smell of soap. She had never been so intensely aware of a man in her life. She was terrified he would somehow guess the effect he had on her, and she gave a silent prayer of thanks when Gino opened his mouth like a little bird and swallowed the medicine without a murmur.

'Good boy,' she said softly as she lifted

him back into her arms and sat him in his highchair.

Raul tore his eyes from the sight of Libby's nipples jutting provocatively beneath her tight-fitting top, incensed by the damnable ache of desire in his gut. 'When can you be ready to leave for Italy?' he demanded tersely.

Libby gave him a panic-stricken glance, startled by his arrogant assumption that she would agree to take Gino to live in another country just because he had demanded it. And it wasn't just the move, she fretted. There was no getting away from the fact that she would be going to Italy under false pretences. She wasn't Gino's mother, and she did not know how she was going to live a lie. But what choice did she have? she wondered as she stared at Raul Carducci's cold eyes.

'I'm not sure,' she murmured evasively. 'I'll have to give my landlord notice that I'm closing the shop, and then I'll have to try and sell off the stock. And of course I'll have to pack.' Not that it would take long to pack up her possessions, Libby knew. Her wardrobe was sparse, to say the least, but she wanted to take all her art materials and her canvases, and the few mementoes she had of her mother. 'I could probably be ready to bring Gino to Italy at the end of the month.'

'I was thinking in terms of days, not weeks,' Raul said coolly. 'My staff will organise clearing the shop and transporting your possessions to Italy. All you need to do is pack a few clothes for you and Gino. That shouldn't take more than an hour.' He drew back his cuff to glance at the gold watch on his wrist. 'I see no reason why we shouldn't leave this afternoon.'

'This afternoon!' Libby's jaw dropped in astonishment. 'Surely you must realise that's impossible? I've a million things to do before I'll be ready to take Gino to another country to start a new life.' The words 'another country' and 'new life' thudded in her head, and fear unfurled inside her. She wasn't sure she wanted a new life. Her life in Pennmar was not easy—especially at the moment, when the shop was doing so badly—but at least it *was* her life, lived on her own terms, rather than a life of pretending to be someone else under Raul Carducci's haughty gaze. 'Anyway, what's the hurry?' she asked him, pushing her tangled red curls over her shoulder. 'What does it matter to you when we come?'

Against the backdrop of the dreary room and the sullen grey sky outside the window Libby's hair seemed as bright and alive as the dancing flames of a fire. In her garish clothes

she was a splash of vibrant colour in a black
and white world, Raul mused, as startlingly
vivid as the numerous colourful canvases
which were stacked around the room.

He chose not to answer her question. 'Are
these your work?' he asked, glancing around
at the bold pictures of land and seascapes that
seemed almost to leap off the canvases.

'Yes. My favourite mediums are oils and
charcoals.'

Raul studied a painting of a terraced garden
with pots of brilliantly coloured flowers. The
picture was loud and brash, with dashes of
red, orange and purple seemingly flung at the
canvas, yet somehow it worked, and he felt
as though he could reach out and touch the
flowers. 'Do you sell many?'

Libby detected scepticism in his voice
and bristled. 'A few—quite a lot, actually.
Although that was mainly in the summer,
when the tourists were here. I display them
in the shop, but trade is quiet at the moment,'
she admitted dismally.

'You won't have to concern yourself with
making a living once you move into the Villa
Giulietta,' Raul informed her coolly. 'There
will certainly be no need for you to work
as a lap-dancer,' he added, his lip curling
contemptuously.

'Well, that's lucky, because I've never worked as a lap-dancer,' Libby snapped, feeling hot all over when he trailed his eyes insolently down her body and lingered quite blatantly on her breasts.

'The Purple Pussy Cat Club?' he drawled.

Libby's face burned even hotter. Evidently Raul had learned about the seedy club where she and Liz had once worked, and now he thought that she had been a lap-dancer. The pitfalls of pretending to be Gino's mother were already becoming apparent. 'I...I wasn't a lap-dancer,' she mumbled, unable to meet his sardonic gaze. 'I worked behind the bar, that's all.'

Her dream of going to art college had been crushed by the reality of having to earn a living. Having left school with few qualifications, she had found her career choices limited, and she had worked as a cleaner and at a fast food outlet before her mum had helped her get a job serving behind the bar at the nightclub where Liz had already worked as a lap-dancer.

It had been the only job her mum could get when they had arrived back in England after spending several years living in Ibiza. Liz had hated it—but, as she had reminded Libby, they needed the money, and anything was better than signing on for unemployment benefit. Her mum had been unconventional, and often irresponsible, but she had also been fiercely proud.

Raul was still staring at her, and something in his eyes sent a ripple of sensation through Libby. She couldn't look away from him. It was as though he had cast a spell over her which rooted her to the spot as he strolled nearer, those midnight-dark eyes boring into her as if he were looking into her soul.

He halted inches from her, and almost as if he could not help himself he reached out and wrapped a silky red curl around his finger. 'So, you're not a stripper?'

'*No!*' Her face felt like a furnace, but she was trapped by his magnetism and seemed incapable of moving away from him.

His brows rose and he looked down his arrogant nose at her. 'Pity,' he murmured. 'I might have considered paying you for a private performance.'

'Well, you would have wasted your money,' Libby snapped, her will-power finally reasserting itself so that she jerked away from him. She lifted Gino out of his highchair and hugged him to her. 'I don't think this is going to work. I'm not sure I want to bring Gino to Italy to live at the Carducci villa—certainly not if you're going to make comments like that. Anyway,' she added, desperately clutching at reasons why they should not go with Raul, 'I can't come with you now. Gino has an appointment with a paediatrician next week because my GP is concerned about his respiratory problems.'

Raul had moved back to the window and was staring at the rain, which was now lashing the glass. 'Of course you'll come. You're not going to turn down the opportunity to live a life of luxury,' he drawled confidently. He glanced back at Libby and tried to ignore the burning ache in his groin. Clearly he'd been too long without a lover if he could be attracted to his father's tart, he derided himself. It was a situation he would remedy once he returned home. He could take his pick from numerous beautiful, sophisticated women who understood that all he wanted was a casual sexual relationship with no strings attached.

But first it was imperative that he persuaded Elizabeth Maynard to return to Italy with him immediately. Much as he resented the fact, she controlled fifty percent of Carducci Cosmetics, and he could not run the company without her. 'Once we are in Italy I will arrange for the baby to see a private specialist,' he assured her. 'Gino is a Carducci, and I know his father would have wanted him to have the best of everything.'

The best of everything—the words echoed in Libby's head. Wasn't that what her mother would have wanted for Gino, too? She stared around the flat, at the threadbare carpet and the patches of damp on the walls, and bit her lip, conscious that Raul was watching her.

'How can you deny Gino his birthright?' he demanded. 'Already the spring sunshine in Lazio is warming the lake beside the Villa Giulietta, and the warm climate will be good for him. As he grows older he will have the run of the house and grounds. He can play in the orange groves and learn to sail on the lake.' He would teach his father's son, just as Pietro had taught *him* to sail when he had been a boy, Raul vowed silently.

A thought suddenly struck him that might mean an annoying delay to his plans to take his father's son to Italy as soon as possible. 'I don't suppose Gino has a passport?'

'Actually, he does,' Libby replied slowly. Her mother had applied for one soon after Gino had been born. It had been most unlike Liz to be so organised, but Libby guessed that her mum had hoped Pietro would send for her and his baby son. Liz would have wanted

Gino to live in Italy, in a grand house rather than this flat, she knew.

To her surprise Raul did not sound as though he resented his baby half-brother, as she had first feared, and actually seemed to *want* Gino to live at the Carducci villa.

She thought of the bank's refusal to increase her overdraft, and the worry that had kept her awake for the past few nights of how she was going to pay the next month's rent on the shop and flat. The truth was that she was at rock-bottom, and there was a very real danger that she and Gino would be homeless. Pietro Cardicci's will was nothing short of a miracle which assured Gino's financial security for life. As Raul had pointed out, she did not have the right to deny Gino his birthright. And Raul had promised he would arrange for Gino to see a private specialist about his dreadful cough...

'All right,' she said abruptly, her heart thumping. She felt as though she was about to jump over the edge of a precipice into the unknown, but Gino had been offered the chance of a better life than the one she could give him in Pennmar, and for his sake she *had* to take it. 'We'll come with you today.'

'Good.' Satisfaction laced Raul's voice. He had never doubted that the lure of the

Carducci fortune would persuade Libby to move to Italy. He strolled across the room and lifted Gino out of her arms. 'I'll hold him while you pack. My private jet is on stand-by at Newquay airport. I'll tell the pilot to be ready to take off two hours from now.'

CHAPTER THREE

'WE SHOULD arrive at the Villa Giulietta in a few minutes,' Raul announced abruptly.

Libby had been staring out of the car window, watching the Italian countryside flash past, but at the sound of his rich-as-clotted-cream voice she turned her head and felt a peculiar tightening sensation in the pit of her stomach when she glanced at his handsome face. He possessed a simmering sexual magnetism that fascinated her, and she could not prevent herself from staring at his mouth, imagining the feel of it on hers. Raul's kiss would be no gentle seduction. The thought slid into her head, and she was shocked to feel a hot, melting sensation between her legs.

Her face burned with embarrassment and she prayed he could not read her mind. How could she feel such a fierce attraction to a man she disliked intensely? But it was no good reminding herself that Raul was the

most arrogant man she had ever met. Her
body seemed to have a mind of its own, and
his closeness, the subtle tang of his cologne,
made each of her nerve-endings thrum with
urgent life.

Her reaction was probably caused by shock
that he had finally deigned to speak to her
after he had ignored her throughout the flight
to Italy, she decided irritably. Back in her flat
in Pennmar she had hastily packed Gino's
clothes and her own few belongings. When
she had walked back into the living room
Raul had compressed his lips at the sight of
her bright orange coat, and his disdainful
comment, 'You seem to be wearing just about
every colour of the rainbow,' had made her
wish that she owned elegant, sophisticated
clothes rather than oddments she'd picked up
from charity shops.

He was so stuffy, she thought rebelliously.
He couldn't be more than in his mid-thirties,
but he had a way of looking down his nose at
her, just as Mr Mills—the headmaster of the
secondary school she had attended intermit-
tently—had done when he had told her that
she would never amount to much.

Maybe all upper-class men acted like
stuffed shirts? Miles certainly had, she
brooded, recalling her brief relationship with

Miles Sefton, which had come to an abrupt end when she had overheard him assuring his father, Earl Sefton, that of *course* his relationship with a waitress from the golf club wasn't serious; she was just a bit of totty.

The memory of that humiliating episode made Libby squirm. Why on earth had she agreed to come to Italy with Raul? she wondered, casting a furtive glance at his chiselled features. He made Earl Sefton seem like Father Christmas. Tears stung her eyes as she remembered how Miles's father had stated that she was little Miss Nobody from Nowhere. Now Miss Nobody was going to live in a grand villa with a man who despised her, and, although she would rather die than show it, she was scared stiff at the prospect.

Lost in her thoughts, Libby had not noticed that the car had slowed, but now it turned and purred up a sweeping driveway lined with tall cypress trees. Through the dark green foliage she glimpsed tantalising flashes of pink and cream stone, while in the distance she caught the sparkle of sunshine on blue water. She remembered Raul had said the villa was near a lake, and suddenly the line of trees stopped, the driveway opened out onto a wide courtyard—and her jaw dropped in astonishment as she stared at the most beautiful house she had ever seen.

'*Wow...*' she said faintly. The Villa Giulietta looked like a fairytale castle, with its four rounded turrets and myriad arched windows glinting gold in the evening sunlight. The pink and cream striped brickwork reminded Libby of a candy-stick, while the ornate stonework at the top of the turrets was exquisitely detailed.

The courtyard ran round to the front of the house, which overlooked an enormous sapphire-blue lake. A series of stone steps led up to the front door, and cream and pink roses grew in profusion over the elegant stone pillars of the porch.

'It's...incredible,' she murmured, utterly overwhelmed by the house's splendour.

'I agree.' For a moment Raul forgot the anger and frustration that had simmered inside him since he had read Pietro's will, forgot that the woman at his side had been his father's mistress who now had the right to live at the villa. This was his home and he loved it.

His ex-wife had accused him of caring more about the house than he had about her—particularly when he had refused to move permanently to New York. By then his marriage to Dana had been in its death throes and he hadn't denied it. When they had separated he'd offered her the Manhattan apartment, believing that she would not make a claim on the villa.

How wrong he had been, Raul thought bitterly. Dana had proved to be an avaricious gold-digger. Their divorce had made legal history when she had won a record alimony settlement after only a year of marriage. But although it had cost him a fortune he had at least forced her to relinquish her claim on the Villa Giulietta, and the experience had taught him that marriage was a fool's game which he had no intention of ever repeating.

As the car drew to a halt, a woman appeared at the top of the steps and watched them alight. Libby guessed her to be in her mid-sixties; whippet-thin and elegantly dressed, she did not move forward to greet them but waited imperiously for Raul to come to her.

'My aunt Carmina,' Raul murmured to Libby, before he strode up the steps.

'*Zia* Carmina.' He stifled his impatience as he took his aunt's hand and lifted it briefly to his lips. She was his mother's sister, he reminded himself. His father had been fond of her and had often invited her to stay at the villa. Raul knew that Carmina had had been deeply upset by Pietro's death, but she seemed determined to ignore his gentle hints that she might like to return to her house in Rome, and his sympathy was wearing thin.

Gino had woken when the car had stopped moving, and he gave Libby a gummy grin when she lifted him out of his seat. Feeling overawed by the magnificent house, she hovered uncertainly at the bottom of the steps, her heart sinking when Raul's aunt subjected her to a haughty stare that grew gradually more incredulous.

'Who is this woman?' Carmina demanded in Italian.

Raul gestured for Libby to join him. 'This is Elizabeth Maynard,' he replied in English. 'She was my father's…' He hesitated, conscious of the scandalised expression on *Zia* Carmina's face as she raked her eyes over Libby's wild red curls and garishly coloured clothes. For some reason he was reluctant to refer to Libby as Pietro's mistress, but his aunt had transferred her gaze to Gino and she threw up her hands in a gesture of disgust.

'This *girl* was my brother-in-law's mistress?' Again she spoke in voluble Italian. 'She looks so common. What was Pietro thinking? He must have been out of his mind to have invited his *puttana* to live at the Villa Giulietta.'

Raul had felt exactly the same sentiments, but now he felt a shaft of annoyance with his aunt for her rudeness, and was glad that Libby could not understand what she had said. 'My father was entitled to do as he wished, and he made it clear that he wished for his…companion and his infant son to live here,' he reminded the older woman coolly.

'Pah!' Carmina made no attempt to greet Libby, and after giving her another disdainful glance swung round and swept back into the house.

Libby watched her go and hugged Gino to her, startled to find that her hands were shaking. She hadn't followed any of the lightning-fast exchange between Raul and his aunt, but the older woman's sentiments had been plain. *Puttana* probably meant something vile, she brooded as she recalled how Carina had practically spat the word at her.

Once again she questioned her sanity in pretending to be Gino's mother. Perhaps the Carducci family would be more prepared to accept her if she explained that Pietro had not been her sugar-daddy? But if Raul learned that she had no right to remain at the villa he might order his chauffeur to drive her straight back to the airport.

He could not physically snatch Gino from her, she assured herself, automatically tightening her hold on the baby. But this was a man who travelled by private jet and lived in a villa that looked like a palace. His wealth and the power he commanded were undeniable, and she was sure that if he decided to fight for custody of Gino he would win.

The baby was heavy, and she transferred him to her other hip. 'Here—let me take him,' Raul offered, holding out his hands.

'No!' She gripped Gino convulsively, blushing when Raul frowned. 'Thanks, but he doesn't really know you, and I don't want to unsettle him while he's getting used to a strange house,' she muttered.

Raul stared at her speculatively. 'I'm sure he'll soon get used to me—and the house.'

He wondered why Libby seemed so nervous. Most women he knew would be unable to conceal their delight at the prospect of living at the villa with all expenses paid, but she looked as though she had been sentenced to a term in jail. She made an incongruous sight in her purple boots and skirt, green tights and orange coat, but nothing could detract from the loveliness of her face. His eyes focused on her soft mouth, and he could not banish the image of covering her lips with his own in a long, leisurely tasting.

Dio, she was a witch, he thought furiously as he moved abruptly away from her. 'Follow me. I'll show you to your rooms,' he ordered curtly.

Wordlessly Libby trailed after him, her misgivings increasing as she stepped into the hall and stared around at the marble floors and pillars and the exquisite murals which adorned the walls and ceiling. Rays of early evening sunlight slanted through the windows and danced across the stunning crystal chandelier suspended from the centre of the room. She would have liked to linger and study the beautiful bronze sculptures dotted around the hallway, but Raul was striding ahead and she had to race to keep up with him.

He led the way along endless corridors, past elegant, airy rooms filled with antique furniture. She could easily spend the rest of her life lost in these corridors, Libby fretted as she followed him up yet another flight of stairs. Raul suddenly stopped and pushed open a door, before standing back to usher her into a suite of rooms that comprised a sitting room, small dining area and an adjoining bedroom.

'I have arranged for this room to be the nursery,' he told Libby, opening another door into a smaller room which had been decorated in soft yellow. The stripped-pine cot and nursery furniture were attractive, and the pale blue striped curtains and matching rug on the floor added to the ambience of the room.

Libby set Gino down on the floor and he immediately crawled over to the box of brightly coloured toys in the corner. Raul watched him for a few moments before commenting, 'He doesn't seem too unsettled, does he? The nanny has the room next door to this one, by the way,' he added casually.

Libby stared at him. 'What nanny?'

'The one I have hired to help take care of Gino. She comes from the best agency in Italy and is highly recommended.'

'I don't care if she's Mother Teresa.' Fear sharpened Libby's voice. She did not want anyone to take her place in Gino's life. 'You can just *un*-hire her,' she snapped. 'I'm perfectly capable of looking after him myself.'

Raul's brows rose in an expression of haughty disdain. 'From what I saw of your flat in Pennmar, I disagree. It was a filthy hovel.'

Outraged by his description of her former home, Libby felt her temper explode. 'It was *not* filthy. I was always cleaning, and scrubbing the mildew off the walls. It's not my fault the flat was so damp.'

'The living room looked like a pigsty,' Raul insisted coldly.

'That was only because I'd had to move all my things out of my bedroom when it flooded—' Libby broke off at the sound of a knock on the door and stared suspiciously at the dark-haired woman who entered the room.

'Ah, Silvana.' Raul stepped forward to greet the woman. 'I'd like to introduce you to your new charge.' He scooped Gino into his arms, and to Libby's annoyance the baby chuckled happily and explored Raul's face with his hand. 'This is Gino.' Raul paused, and then as an obvious afterthought added, 'Oh—and his mother, Ms Maynard.'

Silvana gave Libby a cheerful smile and immediately turned her attention to Gino. 'What a gorgeous little boy,' she said in perfect English, and then in Italian, '*Sei un bel bambino*, Gino.'

'He doesn't understand Italian,' Libby said tightly, wishing that Gino had yelled when the nanny had spoken to him. But he seemed quite content in Raul's arms, and was giving Silvana his most winsome smile—the smile he usually only gave *her*, Libby thought dismally.

'Silvana is fluent in English and Italian, and she will talk to Gino in both languages so that he will grow up bilingual,' Raul informed Libby coolly. 'Italy is his home now, and obviously he will need to be fluent in his native tongue—don't you agree?'

'I suppose so,' Libby muttered. Of course Gino would need to be able to speak Italian, she just hadn't thought of it, and she was irritated that Raul was one step ahead. 'I'll have to learn too. I picked up Spanish fairly easily, so I guess Italian won't be too hard.'

'Did you learn Spanish at school?' Raul asked curiously.

'No...' Libby did not want to admit that she'd received no formal schooling until she and her mum had left Ibiza and returned to live in London, or that her attendance at the local comprehensive had been sketchy and she had learned very little. 'I spent part of my childhood in Ibiza and learned to speak Spanish there.'

She frowned when Raul gave Gino to the nanny, surprised that the baby did not remonstrate at being handed to a stranger. He was obviously growing out of his clingy stage, and it was selfish to wish that he only wanted her, she told herself firmly.

'Would you like me to give Gino his tea and a bath?' Silvana asked.

Libby opened her mouth to argue, but thought better of it when she noticed Raul's steely expression. When he opened the door and ushered her into the adjoining room she stalked past him, and as soon as they were out of earshot of Silvana she rounded on him.

'I can't stop you employing a nanny, but you're wasting your money—because *I* am Gino's mother and *I* will be his full-time carer, just as I have always been.'

Raul was surprised by her fierceness. He had convinced himself that Libby had deliberately conceived Pietro's child in the hope of claiming a huge maintenance allowance, and had assumed that she would be more than happy to hand over responsibility for her baby. But during the flight to Italy he had been struck by her devotion to Gino and her obvious love for him. 'You can't have cared for him entirely on your own in England when you had the shop to run,' he pointed out. 'You say you are an artist, but looking after a baby can't have given you much time to paint.'

Libby shrugged. 'I used to take him down

to the shop with me. And I painted whenever Gino had a nap. But I've pretty much
given up my artwork since…' She had been
about to say since *Mum had Gino*, but quickly
changed that to, 'Since Gino was born.'

Raul thought of the bold, beautiful paintings he had seen at her flat. 'That must
have been hard—to give up something you
love?'

Libby slipped off her coat and brushed her
tangled red curls back from her face. 'Not
really. Gino comes first. I love him more than
anything,' she said fiercely.

Raul compressed his lips and walked over
to the window, needing to look anywhere
but at Libby. Now that she had removed her
coat his eyes once again seemed to have a
magnetic attraction to her breasts. He was
bitterly aware that his body had been in a
state of arousal ever since her soft curves
had squashed up against him in the car. She
was so intense; he brooded, so colourful and
fizzing with energy. Had it been her energy
and her fiery passion that had attracted his
father to her? He pushed the thought away. He
could not bear to think about her and Pietro
as lovers… Not when he wanted her himself,
whispered a sly little voice in his head.

Incensed by his own weakness, he swung

round to face her. 'Like it or not, there will be occasions when you will have to leave Gino with Silvana. You cannot take him to board meetings,' he pointed out when she looked mutinous.

Libby frowned. 'I won't be going to any board meetings...will I?' she asked uncertainly.

'As I have explained, my father has left a fifty percent share of Carducci Cosmetics to Gino. But until he is eighteen *you* have control of his share of the company, and it will be necessary for you to attend meetings with the board of directors.'

'I see.' Libby chewed on her bottom lip, horrified at the prospect of discussing business matters with the board members of Carducci Cosmetics, who would no doubt look down their noses at her just as Raul was doing now. 'I don't really know a lot about running a company,' she admitted.

'That much was obvious from the precarious financial state of your shop,' Raul said scathingly. 'Do not fear. You won't have to do anything apart from sign your name where I tell you to.'

Libby glared at him resentfully, infuriated by his implication that she had mismanaged the shop when she had worked so hard to make Nature's Way a success. 'I suppose I'll have to leave Gino with the nanny while I attend meetings,' she conceded grudgingly. 'At least Silvana seems pleasant—unlike your aunt.' She grimaced as she recalled Raul's aunt's haughty disdain. Her careless tongue ran away with her and she added, 'She's a miserable old bat.'

Privately, Raul shared Libby's opinion of his aunt. But Carmina was a member of his family, his beloved mother's sister, while Libby had been his father's mistress—a cheap little gold-digger. 'I will not tolerate you speaking about any member of my family so disrespectfully,' he snapped. 'You are here because my father wished it, but I suggest you remember your place.'

His arrogance ignited Libby's temper like a match to dry tinder. 'What exactly *is* my place?' she demanded, throwing back her head so that her flame-coloured curls danced around her face. 'Your precious aunt looked at me as if I had crawled out of the gutter. And what does *puttana* mean, by the way? Maybe I'll ask Silvana to translate for me.'

Raul glared at her furiously. Never in his life had anyone challenged his authority or spoken to him in such a way as Libby had. He was tempted to grab hold of her and bring his mouth down on hers in a punishing kiss that would shut her up. His nostrils flared as he struggled to control his temper, but his eyes were as cold as chips of granite as he met her gaze. 'It means whore,' he said grimly.

'Oh.' Libby's temper deflated like a popped balloon and she felt sick inside. She had been under no illusion that she would be welcomed at the Villa Giulietta. Raul must have been shocked to learn that he was not his father's sole heir, and he clearly resented her, believing as he did that she had been Pietro's mistress. He had accused her of being a gold-digger who had targeted a much older, wealthy man—but a whore! 'That's horrible,' she muttered, tears filling her eyes.

Dio! Libby was a brilliant actress, Raul brooded, infuriated by the pang of guilt that gripped him when he saw her lower lip tremble. She looked so hurt and so achingly vulnerable, but in his experience most women were manipulative, and he was convinced that she was no different.

'*Zia* Carmina was my mother's sister. After Eleanora's death she remained close to my father,' he explained harshly. 'You must understand that my aunt was deeply shocked to learn that her brother-in-law, whom she loved and respected, had had a secret mistress and a child.' He frowned. 'You are so young. *Dio*, Pietro was old enough to have been your grandfather. It is not surprising that Carmina finds your presence here difficult when she is still grieving for my father.'

'Grief doesn't give a person licence to be nasty,' Libby said, rounding on him. 'I'm grieving too.' The pain of losing her mum was still raw. During the day she had to be strong for Gino, but most nights she still cried for Liz. 'These past few months have been the worst of my life,' she told Raul thickly.

Surely Libby was faking the emotion that throbbed in her voice? She could not really be as devastated by his father's death as she appeared? Raul stared at her in frustration, not knowing what to make of her. Before he had met her he had pigeonholed her as a brash tart devoid of any scruples. But Libby was nothing like he had imagined. If she were to be believed, it seemed that she had genuinely cared for Pietro. But why had such a beautiful young woman been attracted to a man forty years older than her if it hadn't been for his money? he asked himself angrily.

Raul tore his gaze from Libby, feeling a sudden need to get away from her. It would have been so much easier if she had been a hard-as-nails bimbo, he thought savagely.

He wanted to despise her, but every time he looked at her he was consumed with a burning sexual hunger that shamed him.

He crossed the room and flipped open a briefcase sitting on the coffee table. 'It has been a long day, and I am sure you want to settle in. Your bag has been brought up from the car and the rest of your things at the flat will be packed up and sent on in a few days.' He lifted a sheaf of documents from the case and glanced at her. 'I need you to sign a few papers.'

'What are they?' Libby stared warily at the pile of printed documents, her heart sinking when she realised that Raul intended to wait while she read them.

'They relate to various decisions I have made regarding Carducci Cosmetics.' Raul flicked casually through the papers. 'This file gives details of a merger with a Swedish skincare company that I want to proceed with as soon as possible, and this document is to authorise the transfer of funds to one of CC's subsidiary companies in the US. I simply require you to sign your name—you don't have to read them.'

Libby frowned. 'How can I sign them when I don't know what I'm signing?

Irritation swept through Raul when she

sat down, switched on the table-lamp, and picked up the first document from the pile. 'This is pointless,' he said grittily, noting how the lamplight turned her hair to spun gold. 'You said yourself you know nothing about running a company. I have no idea why my father stipulated that *you* should have control of Gino's shares,' he burst out, his frustration tangible. 'When Pietro died I expected to take full control of Carducci Cosmetics, but for the past eight months CC has been in a state of limbo. I couldn't find you, and because you control fifty percent of the company I have been unable to do more than keep the company ticking over.' He took a deep breath, calming himself. 'I'm not asking you to take a crash course in business management,' he informed Libby curtly. 'You can save us both a lot of time if you just add your signature to the bottom of each document.'

Libby stared at him, watching how the lamplight flickered over the hard planes of his face. A hard knot of anger was slowly forming inside her at the realisation that he hadn't insisted on rushing her and Gino to Italy because he was concerned about the baby living in the damp flat in Pennmar. No, all Raul cared about was Carducci Cosmetics—which, to his obvious anger, he now had to share control of with her until Gino was eighteen.

'I wonder why Pietro didn't give *you* control of Gino's shares?' she said slowly. 'Maybe he didn't trust that you would look after Gino's interests properly?'

Rage coursed through Raul's veins like red-hot lava flow, obliterating every other thought but the burning need to force an apology from Libby for her outrageous statement. 'You *dare* suggest my father did not trust me?' he snarled, hating her at that moment for echoing the doubts he had secretly harboured since he had read Pietro's will. Maybe she was right; maybe his adoptive father *hadn't* trusted him enough to award him control of Gino's share of the company. The thought tore at his heart, and anger was the only way he could deal with the pain. His nostrils flared with the effort of containing his fury—not just with Libby, but with himself and his shameful, shocking desire for her.

She had gone too far, Libby realised when she risked a glance at Raul's face and saw that his dark eyes were as cold and hard as polished jet. But she wanted the truth. 'Pietro must have had his reasons for stipulating that Gino's mother should control his share of Carducci Cosmetics,' she insisted. And if

Pietro had had his doubts about his adopted son's trustworthiness, then so did she.

Raul jerked his head back as if she had slapped him. '*Dio*, someone needs to teach you to control your insolent tongue,' he growled, goaded beyond bearing.

He moved towards her with the speed of a panther homing in for the kill. Too late Libby realised that he intended the 'someone' to be him, but he had already tangled his fingers in her hair and tugged her head back, and her startled cry was lost beneath the pressure of his mouth as he captured her lips in a savage kiss.

CHAPTER FOUR

LIBBY stiffened; her body taut with rejection as Raul gripped her shoulder and dragged her against him. Shock quickly turned to outrage, and she pressed her lips tightly together and tried to turn her head away. But his strength easily outmatched hers and he tugged her hair, forcing her head back so that he could continue his sensual assault.

For the slide of his lips over hers *was* wickedly sensual, she acknowledged dazedly. It did not matter that she disliked him, or that he clearly despised her. She had fantasised about him kissing her from the moment he had strode into Nature's Way, and the reality of his hot, hungry mouth moving erotically over hers was so intoxicating that she was powerless to deny her response. His tongue probed the firm line of her lips, demanding access, until with a little gasp she opened her mouth and felt a thrill of wild excitement when he slid deep into her moist warmth and explored her with a thoroughness that made her tremble.

Each of her senses was acutely alive, and the taste of him, the scent of him—a tantalising mixture of his cologne and male pheromones—sent fire coursing through her veins. The urge to flee from him was replaced by another instinct: to submit to his superior strength and respond to his hungry demands with a passion she had not known herself capable of. She had never felt like this before— not even with Miles, whom she'd had such a crush on. With one kiss Raul had awoken her sensuality, and now she was eager to experience everything he offered.

She had placed her palms flat on his chest in an effort to push him away, but now she slid her hands up to his shoulders, allowing him to draw her closer. She could feel every sinew and muscle of his thighs and abdomen, and heat pooled between her legs when she felt the hard ridge of his arousal nudge against her pelvis.

His free hand roamed up and down her back, slid over her shoulder and traced the fragile line of her collarbone before moving lower to cup her breast. A quiver of pleasure shot through Libby. Her breasts felt heavy, and her nipples were taut and tingling, straining against the restriction of her lacy bra. She wished he would push his hand beneath the material and stroke her naked flesh. Colour scorched her cheeks at the wantonness of her thoughts, but he was still kissing her with the mastery of a sorcerer, evoking a need in her that caused her to move her body sinuously against his in a blatant invitation.

And then, with shocking abruptness, he ended the kiss and lifted his head to stare down at her for several taut seconds before he jerked away from her, breathing hard. Libby swayed slightly, shaking with reaction and feeling bereft now that his big, hard body was no longer melded to her softer curves.

'That should *not* have happened,' he said harshly.

His voice was laced with self-loathing, and Libby was sure she would see contempt for her in his midnight-dark gaze. Instead his eyes glittered with a feverish hunger that stunned her with its intensity. Raul wanted her. He might hate himself, but for a few unguarded seconds he had been unable to disguise his desire for her.

He had gathered up the sheaf of documents and shoved them back in the briefcase, and was now striding across the room. If he moved any faster he would be running out of the door, she thought, staring in astonishment at the dull colour that highlighted his magnificent cheekbones. She blushed as she recalled how eagerly she had responded to him. Maybe he was afraid she was going to jump on him and drag him back? She remembered the hungry gleam she had seen in his eyes before his thick black lashes had swept down and concealed his thoughts, and it struck her that maybe he was afraid of himself.

Raul grabbed the door handle and jerked the door open with such force that it groaned on its hinges. He was furious with himself—disgusted. *Inferno!* Libby had been his father's mistress and he did not understand how he could want her. He had kissed her in anger, wanting to punish her for suggesting that Pietro had not trusted him. But the punishment had backfired, because from the moment his mouth had claimed her soft, moist lips he had been consumed with a burning need to possess her.

He halted on his way out of the door and glanced back at her, heat searing his insides when he saw that her lips were red and swollen and unutterably tempting. She was a witch, he thought broodingly. A beautiful milky-skinned, doe-eyed sorceress who had ensnared his father—but from now on he would guard himself against her magic.

'I have a prior engagement tonight,' he said coldly, 'and as my aunt has informed me that she is feeling unwell and will not be joining you for dinner I have arranged for your evening meal to be served to you up here in your suite.' He paused, and when she made no reply continued, 'I have called a meeting of all Carducci Cosmetics' senior executives for midday tomorrow. We'll leave for Rome soon after breakfast as I have a number of things to attend to in the office before the meeting. Silvana will look after Gino.'

Libby bit her lip. 'How long will we be away? I don't want to leave him for too long.'

'I imagine the meeting will last for most of the afternoon. There are numerous urgent matters to discuss,' Raul told her with barely concealed impatience, thinking of the months that CC had stagnated while he had searched for his father's mistress. 'We have also been invited to a business dinner in the evening.' He shrugged when Libby frowned. 'Attending these sorts of events is a necessary part of running a company. Social networking is a vital avenue of business.'

He paused and then said smoothly, 'Of

course there *is* a way that you could devote all your time to Gino, and perhaps have time to take up your painting again.'

Libby gave him a puzzled look. 'How?'

'You could sign over control of Gino's shares to me.' Raul spoke savagely when Libby immediately shook her head. '*Dio!* I have spent most of my life preparing to take my father's place as head of CC. Pietro erred on the side of caution, but I have plans for the company that will make it a world leader in the twenty-first century.'

'Maybe your father wished you were *more* cautious,' Libby said slowly. 'Maybe he was worried that you would take too many risks with Carducci Cosmetics, and that's why he stipulated that Gino's mother should have control of his shares until he is an adult. I might not know much about running a company,' she admitted, 'but I'm not stupid. I understand that high risk can mean high returns, but I'm not prepared to gamble with Gino's birthright, and I won't agree to any business ventures that I feel are too risky.'

Black rage swept through Raul. So the battle lines were drawn, he thought bitterly. The only subject he and his father had ever disagreed on was the future of Carducci Cosmetics. Pietro had been content for the company to follow a path of safe investments and carefully considered proposals, while he, Raul, had seen the potential for expansion and diversification. Admittedly they came with risks—but hadn't he proved, by amassing his own personal fortune on the stock market, that his gambles always paid off?

It was clear that his father had not trusted him. By awarding his mistress Gino's shares Pietro had found a way to control Raul from beyond the grave. The only possible solution, Raul realised, lay in the clause Pietro had added to his will stating that if Libby were to marry control of Gino's shares would pass to him. A clause that she was unaware of, because back at her flat in Pennmar she had not bothered to read the will in its entirety, pointed out a little voice in his head.

Madre di Dio! It was such an obvious solution and it would give him what he desired most in the world—complete control of the company he had been groomed to run since he was a boy. But marry his father's mistress? It was absolutely out of the question, he assured himself firmly. The idea was inconceivable. He had experienced the delights of holy matrimony once, Raul thought sardonically, and had no intention of repeating the worst mistake of his life.

Not even if the prize was the thing he desired most in the world? his mind taunted. Not even if it would give him full control of CC and the opportunity to bed a woman who sent his libido into orbit every time he set eyes on her?

He did not envisage any difficulties in persuading Libby to be his wife. She had been willing to have an affair with an elderly billionaire and was not likely to turn down marriage to Pietro's other heir. And of course he would instruct his lawyers to draw up a pre-nup as watertight as a submarine, so that he could divorce her when he tired of her.

He stared across the room at Libby and desire jack-knifed in his gut when he remembered how firm and yet deliciously soft her breast had felt in his hand. He wanted to rip off her clingy top, and the bra he could see outlined beneath it, and cup her naked flesh in his palms, stroke his fingers across her nipples and feel them harden. The chemistry between them was almost tangible. He knew with a primitive instinct that she would not stop him if he carried her into the bedroom and made love to her.

He was unbearably tempted, and it took all his will-power to force himself to step out of her room and close the door behind him. If he married her he could enjoy her delectable body *and* take control of CC. The idea was certainly worth serious consideration.

For several moments after Raul had gone Libby stood with her fingers pressed against her bruised mouth, still reeling from his kiss. How *could* she have responded to him so shamelessly? she berated herself disgustedly. His aunt had accused her of being a whore, and after her wanton behaviour Raul must surely agree with Carmina.

Sudden tears filled her eyes and she sank down onto the sofa and buried her head in her hands. For weeks Gino had woken her every few hours during the night with his cough, and she was so tired she could barely think straight. Today so much had happened in the space of a few short hours that her life seemed scarily out of her control. Raul had stormed into her life with the force of a tornado, but she had agreed to bring Gino to Italy because more than anything she wanted him to have the stability and security that had been lacking in her own childhood.

She had been unprepared for the violent sexual attraction between her and Raul. She knew she was ridiculously inexperienced for a woman of twenty-two—witnessing her mother's disastrous love-life had put her off dating and Miles had been her only serious relationship. But Miles had never made her feel the way Raul had done when he had kissed her.

She could still taste him. She traced her mouth with her fingertips and heat flooded through her when she remembered how he had ground his lips against hers and demanded a response that she had been powerless to deny. For a few seconds she indulged in the fantasy of him kissing her and caressing her, stripping her clothes from her body and pulling her down onto a bed...

Her eyes flew wide-open. That was never going to happen. She could never allow the fantasy to become reality, because Raul believed she was Gino's mother and she could not risk him discovering that she was a virgin. From now on she must ignore the sexual chemistry between them and hope that in the vastness of the Villa Giulietta their paths would not cross very often.

She glanced around the elegant sitting room which, like the bedroom beyond it, was decorated in muted shades and simply begged for splashes of colour to make it feel more homely. The prospect of eating dinner here alone was not inviting, but it was preferable to dining with Raul's unpleasant aunt.

She wondered where Raul would be spending the evening. With his mistress, perhaps? With his stunning looks and potent virility it was likely that he had numerous lovers. But his personal life was none of her business, she reminded herself, irritated because she could not get the image of him making love to some gorgeous woman out of her mind. Forget about Raul Carducci, she told herself. The only person who mattered to her was Gino who was asleep in his airy, *dry* nursery. She had done the right thing by bringing him to live in this beautiful house, and with her mind settled she went to check on him.

The following morning Raul's Lamborghini sped along the roads so fast that the fields and olive groves flashed past in a blur. Libby lifted her eyes from his tanned hands on the steering wheel to his hard profile, and sighed. He had not spoken to her since she had emerged from her bedroom dressed for their trip to Rome, but his silence as he had studied her appearance had thrummed with disapproval.

She did not know what he had expected her to wear, she thought irritably. She didn't own

designer suits, or anything remotely suitable
for a business meeting. Okay, so her denim
mini-skirt was short, but it was perfectly re-
spectable when she was wearing cropped leg-
gings beneath it. Her cerise and purple top
was admittedly pretty eye-catching, but the
pink matched the colour of her flip-flops, and
in an effort to look more elegant she had piled
her hair on top of her head and tied the knot
with a purple scarf.

But in comparison to Raul's superbly tailored charcoal-grey suit, navy blue silk shirt
and grey tie she probably looked a mess,
Libby conceded. He looked every inch a
suave, billionaire businessman, and he was
so drop-dead sexy her stomach lurched every
time he changed gear and his hand brushed
against her thigh.

Desperate to do something to break her
intense awareness of him, she rooted around
in her denim haversack for the tube of mint
sweets she usually carried with her, and eventually unearthed an old packet of chewing
gum. 'Would you like some?' She offered
the packet to Raul.

'You chew *gum*?'

His expression of distaste was almost comi-
cal, but Libby flushed, acutely aware of the
gaping chasm that separated their two worlds.

Presumably the glamorous women he so-cialised with did not chew gum.

'It's not like I take heroin,' she muttered, stuffing the packet back in her bag. 'It's just sugar-free gum.' She shook her head disgust-edly. 'Do you ever lighten up?'

Raul took his eyes from the road for a second and awarded her a sardonic glance. 'If by "lighten up" you mean do I ever dress like a circus clown, then the answer is no.'

'I am not dressed like a circus clown.' Libby breathed fire. 'I simply like to wear bright colours.

'I'd noticed,' he said dryly.

'Well, it's better than being an old fogey. I bet you go to bed wearing a suit.'

'As a matter of fact, I always sleep naked.'

'Oh.' Libby made a choking noise which she quickly tried to disguise as a cough, blushing furiously as an image of Raul—stark naked and reclining on satin sheets—filled her mind.

It was a long time since he had seen a woman blush, Raul mused. But Libby's air of innocence must be an act, he reminded himself, his mouth tightening as he tried to dismiss the recurring image of her and his father as lovers. 'I have a feeling I'm going to regret asking this,' he murmured, 'but what *is* an old fogey? It is not a term I am familiar with.'

'Someone like my old headmaster,' she replied without hesitation. 'Stuffy, pompous, strait-laced…'

'You didn't like him, I take it?' Raul murmured, frowning at the idea that Libby saw him in the same unflattering light as her old schoolmaster. Why should he care what she thought of him? he asked himself impatiently. But her opinion of him rankled. Presumably she hadn't thought him stuffy and strait-laced when she had responded to him so enthusiastically last night.

'Mr Mills didn't like me.' Libby's voice broke into his thoughts. 'He accused me of being a rebel, and told me I wouldn't pass any of my exams. But I proved him wrong,' she said in a satisfied tone. 'I passed art.'

'Just art?' Raul had benefited from an excellent private education at one of Rome's top schools, and gone on to gain a Masters degree in business at Harvard. He could not hide his shock at Libby's lack of qualifications. How was he supposed to share the running of Carducci Cosmetics, which had a seven billion pound annual turnover, with a girl who was barely out of her teens and had a single qualification—in art?

'I assume you were educated in Ibiza, as you said you lived there. Did your parents own property on the island?' he asked her.

'No.' Libby hesitated. There was no reason why she should keep her background a secret, she told herself. 'I was brought up by my mother. I don't have a dad—well, I must do, obviously, but I don't know who he is. He abandoned Mum when she was pregnant with me. Mum was seventeen when I was born and she had a few problems.' She did not add that Liz had taken drugs for several years, or that life on the rundown housing estate where they had lived for the first few years of her life had been grim.

'Social Services eventually placed me with foster parents while Mum sorted her life out. It was fine.' Her voice faltered slightly. 'My foster parents were nice people, but they cared for seven other kids, and life with them was pretty hectic. I missed Mum terribly and I was glad when I was allowed to live with her again. That's when she took me to Ibiza, to live in a commune with artists and free-thinkers.'

For free-thinkers read hippies, Raul thought sardonically. Libby had clearly had an unconventional upbringing—the child of an unmarried mother and now a single parent herself. He hoped she did not harbour any ideas of taking Gino to live in a commune, because he would not allow it, he vowed. His father's son belonged at the Villa Giulietta. Raul suddenly realised he was glad Pietro had stipulated that the baby should grow up at the villa, where he would be safe.

Another thought occurred to him. If he married Libby, he could adopt Gino and claim custody of him should his mother decide to take off and live in an artists' commune. He forced the idea to the back of his mind and concentrated on the road that was filling with traffic as they headed towards the city centre. 'So, how long did you live in the commune?'

'Seven years. We went back to England when I was fourteen,' Libby explained. 'I'd had a few lessons from one of the commune members who had been a teacher, but when I went to the local secondary school in London I soon realised there were big gaps in my knowledge. I'd been allowed to run wild in Ibiza,' she admitted. 'I wasn't used to formal education, and I hated the lessons and the uniform.' And, even worse, the feeling that she was a failure, she reflected silently. 'The only subject I shone at was art.'

Now that she was an adult she bitterly regretted her poor education. She had adored her mother, but she knew that Liz had often been irresponsible—particularly when she had failed to provide proper schooling for Libby.

But she would still rather have lived with her mother than anyone else. Going into care had been a traumatic experience, which was why, after Liz had died, she had been so determined to keep Gino. He belonged to her, she thought fiercely. Raul was legally Gino's half-brother, but because Raul was Pietro's adopted son, he and Gino were not blood relatives, and he would never love the baby as she did.

Lost in her thoughts, she suddenly realised that Raul was speaking. 'How do you think you are going to be able to take an active role in running Carducci Cosmetics when you've admitted you have no business experience?' he demanded impatiently. 'Pietro must have been out of his mind when he awarded you control of Gino's shares. A lap-dancer with a qualification in art—' He broke off and growled something in Italian that Libby guessed was not complimentary.

'I may not have tons of qualifications, but I learned to be streetwise from an early age,' Libby retaliated. 'For years I used to help Mum run a market stall, and I'm confident I can tell the difference between a dodgy deal and a safe one. I'm determined to look after Gino's interests to the best of my ability, and keep his shares in the company safe. And I already told you I never worked as a lap-dancer,' she added tightly.

'So where did you meet my father?'

The question came out of the blue, and Libby froze, frantically trying to recall everything Liz had told her about her holiday romance with Pietro Carducci.

'We met on a cruise ship,' she mumbled. 'The *Aurelia*. It was a month-long trip, visiting ports around the Mediterranean.'

She could sense Raul's surprise. 'Do you often take cruises?'

Libby was not a natural liar, and she could feel her cheeks grow hot as she became more embroiled in the deception she had started when she had told Raul she was Gino's mother. 'No—it was my first cruise. I won the trip in a competition,' she added, relieved that that part of the story was true. Liz had been ecstatic when she had won the luxury holiday.

'So, you met my father on the ship?' Raul drawled. He remembered from when he had escorted Pietro aboard the *Aurelia* that most of the other guests had been elderly. Beautiful young Libby must have had rich pickings, he thought cynically.

'Yes.' Libby recounted her mother's story of how she had met Pietro. 'The *Aurelia* was huge. I took a wrong turn on my way back to my cabin one evening and ended up on the first-class deck. Pietro was returning to his suite, we got chatting, and…well,' she finished lamely, 'that's how we met.'

'It was certainly a fortuitous wrong turn you took that night,' Raul commented silkily.

Libby flushed at his sardonic tone. It was clear he believed his father had been targeted by a calculating gold-digger. But her mum hadn't been like that, she thought miserably. Liz had brought her up alone after being abandoned by Libby's father. Life had been tough, but Liz had been fiercely independent and would never have been attracted to a man for his money. Yet it would be impossible to explain that to Raul, Libby knew—especially as she had led him to believe that *she* had been his father's mistress. She had dug herself a hole and now she was falling ever deeper into it, but if she wanted to stay with Gino she could never reveal the truth.

Raul compressed his lips into an angry line, but did not say any more as he slotted the Lamborghini into his reserved parking space outside Carducci Cosmetics' office block. The building was a modern confection of steel, tinted windows and grey marble steps leading up to the front doors; the foyer was discreetly elegant, with marble pillars, black leather sofas and a reception desk staffed by women who looked as though they had stepped from the pages of *Vogue*.

She should definitely have worn make-up, Libby realised, after the lift had whisked them up to the top floor, where they were met by Raul's ultra-glamorous PA. Power-dressing and scarlet lipstick were clearly *de rigueur* for the female staff at CC, and when Raul ushered her into the boardroom she was conscious that her unconventional clothes drew glances of shocked disapproval from the eight male executives seated around the table.

Four hours later Libby had to concede that running a global company which boasted an annual revenue of several billion pounds and employed twenty thousand staff worldwide was nothing like selling souvenirs to tourists from a market stall in Ibiza.

Her head ached from trying to understand the discussions that had taken place—even though, out of deference to her, everyone had spoken in English rather than Italian. Now, finally, the meeting was over, and she closed her eyes wearily—but snapped them open again at the sound of Raul's terse voice.

'I realise you find the proceedings boring, but I'd appreciate it if you could at least remain conscious during a meeting.'

She flushed at his sarcasm. 'I wasn't bored, and I certainly didn't fall asleep, but I admit I didn't understand most of what was discussed.'

'Then for pity's sake sign over control of Gino's shares to me and allow me to get on with running CC,' Raul bit out savagely, his eyes darkening with fury when she shook her head. Jaw tense, he tore his gaze from Libby and resisted the urge to brush a stray flame-coloured curl off her face.

'Tonight's function starts at eight, which means you have plenty of time to find something suitable to wear,' he told her as he ushered her out of the boardroom and into the lift. 'Many of the top designer boutiques are in Via Condotti and Piazza di Spagna,' he added as the lift doors opened at the ground floor. 'I'll take you to your appointment with the personal stylist, but I'm due at another meeting so I will have to leave you with her.'

'Whoa!' Libby exclaimed as she raced across the marble foyer, trying to keep up with Raul's long stride. 'I don't need a personal stylist.'

He turned his head and ran his eyes slowly over her, from her unruly red curls, huge purple hoop earrings and psychedelic top, down to her minuscule skirt and shudderingly awful pink rubber flip-flops. And to his intense frustration realised that he still wanted her more than he had wanted any other woman. 'You most certainly do,' he assured her grimly. 'You are a representative of Carducci Cosmetics now, and I will not allow you to attend a prestigious dinner looking like someone who scrubs floors for a living.'

Two hours later, Raul strode into the five-star hotel where the dinner was to be held, and made his way to the bar where he had told Libby to meet him.

He might have known she would be late, he thought irritably as he glanced around the room and failed to spot anyone wearing a garishly coloured outfit. Presumably the queen of clashing colours would appear at any moment. He had explained to her that when she had finished shopping Tito, his driver, would take her back to his penthouse apartment so that she could change for the dinner, before the chauffer drove her to the hotel. So where was she? he wondered impatiently, when a glance at his watch revealed that it was ten minutes past the time he had arranged to meet her.

He moved his gaze slowly along the line of people sitting on stools by the bar, and his attention was caught by a shimmer of amethyst silk. The woman had her back to him, but as he lifted his eyes from the silver stiletto heels visible below her long skirt, up to her to her slender waist, and then higher to her milky-pale shoulders revealed by her strapless dress, he felt a jolt of stunned recognition. Her flame-coloured hair had been cleverly tamed and smoothed into loose, silky curls that rippled down her back, but he was not mistaken: it was Libby.

Hot, primitive desire kicked in Raul's gut as he stared at her reflection in the mirror behind the bar. Her make-up was discreet— just a hint of smoky grey eyeshadow which brought out the colour of her stunning blue-green eyes, a slick of mascara to define her long lashes, and a rose-pink gloss on her lips. The dress was a masterpiece of understated elegance that he knew would have come with an exorbitant price tag, but it was worth every penny, he decided, feeling himself harden as he noted how the superb cut of the bodice displayed her breasts like plump, velvety peaches.

Libby was naturally beautiful, but tonight she looked exquisite—and so incredibly sexy that his mouth ran dry as he strode over to the bar. She had dominated his thoughts and caused his body to be in a permanent state of arousal since he had first set eyes on her. Now he was not prepared to fight his urgent desire for her any longer.

CHAPTER FIVE

'CAN I get you a drink, *Signorina?*'

The barman gave Libby a polite smile, but it did not escape her notice that his eyes lingered boldly on the low-cut neckline of her dress. She was tempted to order an orange juice. At least holding the glass would give her something to do with her hands, and perhaps stop her feeling so horribly self-conscious while she waited for Raul. But as she was about to speak a familiar voice sounded from behind her.

'The lady will have champagne.'

It was a voice that never failed to send a quiver of reaction down her spine, as rich and sensuous as molten chocolate, and Libby's heart jolted painfully beneath her ribs as she turned her head and met Raul's dark gaze. His eyes gleamed like polished jet, and yet they seemed different, she noticed dazedly, no longer as cold as pools of black ice, but warm, and glinting with a sensual promise that trapped her breath in her throat.

'Raul,' she greeted him uncertainly, her voice emerging in a whispery breath, while a curious achy sensation unfurled in the pit of her stomach. No man had ever looked at her the way Raul was doing, and she had never expected *him*, of all men, to stare at her with such scorching desire blazing in his eyes.

'*Sei bellissima!*' he murmured in a velvet soft tone that brought her skin out in goosebumps. 'You look amazing in that dress, *cara*.'

She was drowning in his liquid gaze and had to moisten her lips with her tongue before she could speak. 'This old thing?' She resorted to flippancy in a frantic attempt to hide the effect he had on her. 'It's just something I slipped on to scrub the floor.'

Amusement glinted in his eyes, but to her amazement his smile was rueful. 'I can't believe I said that. You would look beautiful wearing sackcloth,' he astounded her by saying. 'But in that dress…' He moved his eyes slowly over her, leaving a trail of heat in his wake. 'You blow me away, *bella*.'

Not knowing quite what to make of this new Raul, who was no longer looking at her as if she were the most repugnant creature on the planet, Libby took a sip of champagne. It was deliciously cool and crisp, and she giggled as the bubbles exploded on her tongue. 'I've never tried champagne before,' she confessed, her pleasure fading when he looked amused. She bit her lip. 'But you already know that I'm not sophisticated, like the other women here tonight,' she said in a low tone.

Raul's smile faded and he stared at her intently. 'You are the most vibrant person I have ever met,' he admitted truthfully. 'You make me feel more alive than I have ever felt, and I regret that you find me stuffy.'

'I don't,' she denied swiftly, lifting her head so that their eyes locked. The electricity in the air around them was almost tangible and she knew that he felt it as strongly as she. She did not know what had happened during the two hours while he had attended a meeting and she had been bullied by a glamorous personal stylist into buying a whole wardrobe of exorbitantly expensive clothes; all she knew was that Raul was no longer looking at her with anger and resentment in his eyes. Incredibly, they no longer seemed to be enemies, they were simply a man and woman drawn together by the mysterious alchemy of sexual desire.

'I'm glad to hear it,' he murmured, moving imperceptibly closer, so that she breathed in the tantalising scent of his cologne. She caught her breath when he ran his finger lightly down her cheek. 'I have been thinking that for Gino's sake we should make the effort to be friends. What do you think, *cara*?'

Friends! She could not conceal her surprise. The word conjured up an image of a comfortable, relaxed relationship, like the one she had shared with Tony back in Pennmar. But she could not ever imagine feeling relaxed with Raul. He dominated her senses and made her so intensely aware of his raw masculinity that she could think of little else other than her longing for him to kiss her again.

Utterly disconcerted that he seemed to be offering an olive branch, she watched him sip his champagne, unaware of the wistful expression in her eyes as she stared at his mouth. 'I think friends sounds a good idea. For Gino's sake, of course,' she added hurriedly. An unwelcome thought forced its way into her mind. 'That doesn't mean that I will hand over control of Gino's share of Carducci Cosmetics to you.'

'Of course not,' Raul assured her smoothly.

'I'm still determined to protect Gino's interests,' she warned him.

'I do not doubt your devotion to your son, and I understand your desire to do your best for him.' Raul's sexy smile stole her breath and melted the last vestiges of her resistance. 'I hope that in time you will come to trust me and realise that I want to build on CC's success for Gino's sake.' He touched his champagne flute to hers. 'Let us drink a toast, Libby. To a new beginning.'

She obediently took a sip of champagne, but the subject that had been bothering her since Raul had left her with Maria, the personal stylist, seemed likely to scupper their newfound friendship. 'This dress cost an absolute fortune,' she told him anxiously. 'Not to mention all the other clothes Maria the stylist insisted I needed. She explained that the bill was to be charged to your account, but I have no way of paying you back. The money I have in my savings account won't even cover one shoe,' she observed ruefully, glancing down at the exquisite three-inch stiletto heels that the personal stylist had selected for her to wear with the amethyst silk evening gown.

The shopping trip, during which Maria had whisked her into one designer boutique after another, had seemed surreal—especially as Libby had only ever bought her clothes in charity shops or discount stores. The shopping had been followed by a visit to a hair salon and beauty parlour, and later, when she had changed into the dress at Raul's luxurious penthouse apartment, the feeling that she had fallen into the pages of a fairytale had intensified.

Raul frowned. 'I have already explained that as you are now a representative of CC it is necessary for you to dress appropriately. You do not have to worry about paying for the clothes. Under the terms of my father's will all your personal expenses will be met by Pietro's estate.'

Guilt surged up inside Libby at Raul's words. It was bad enough that she was living at the villa under false pretences, but ten times worse to know that she was not entitled to a penny of the Carducci fortune. She bit her lip. 'I just don't feel comfortable about it,' she mumbled. 'It's fine that Gino's living expenses will be covered, but I feel it is morally wrong for me to live off Pietro's money.'

It was in Raul's mind to point out that it had been morally wrong of Libby to have had an affair with a wealthy man four decades older than her, particularly as he was convinced that Gino's conception had not been an accident. And yet her reluctance to allow him to pay for her clothes seemed genuine. Most women he knew would have been more than happy to flex his credit card, and he felt slightly irritated that Libby was not acting like the gold-digger he had assumed her to be.

He glanced at his watch, aware that the crowd in the bar was thinning as guests began to make their way to the banqueting hall. 'It's time to go in to dinner,' he said, proffering his arm to help her down from the stool.

'How many people will be at this dinner?' Libby asked nervously, gripping his arm as she struggled to balance on her vertiginous heels while he escorted her out of the bar and along a corridor towards a set of double doors which stood open to reveal long rows of white damask-covered tables set with gleaming silver cutlery and crystal glasses.

'Tonight's event is an international trade dinner, and I imagine a couple of hundred guests have been invited.' Raul glanced down at her tense face. 'What's the matter? You look as though you're about to be thrown to the lions.'

Libby bit her lip. 'People are looking at me,' she muttered. 'Do you think they know who I am—?' She broke off, flushing beneath Raul's sardonic glance.

'If you mean do they know that you were my father's mistress and the mother of his illegitimate child then, no, I have not advertised that fact,' he told her coolly. He had been conscious of the interested glances Libby was attracting, particularly from other men, and a primitive, possessive instinct made him move closer to her. 'People are looking, because your flame-coloured hair and English rose complexion make you very noticeable, *cara*. And in that dress you are incredibly beautiful.'

He meant it, Libby was stunned to realise, her heart racing when she glimpsed the raw hunger in Raul's eyes. No man had ever told her she was beautiful before, but as she caught sight of her reflection in one of the huge wall mirrors she could see that the amethyst silk dress suited her colouring and flattered her figure. It was almost impossible to believe that the elegant woman with the mane of tamed, silky curls tumbling down her back was really her, and without thinking she murmured, 'I wish Miles could see me now.'

Raul's dark eyebrows winged upwards. 'Who is Miles?'

'Miles Sefton—only son of Lord Sefton.' Libby grimaced. 'We met when I worked as a waitress at a very exclusive golf club where Miles was a member. I stupidly fell in love with him, and even more stupidly believed him when he said he loved me.'

'But something happened to make you realise he was not in love with you?' Raul murmured. The fact that Libby had been attracted to a member of the English aristocracy was more proof of her gold-digger tendencies. He must have imagined the note of hurt in her voice when she spoke of this Miles Sefton.

Libby nodded. 'When Miles invited me to lunch at Sefton Hall I thought it was because he wanted me to meet his family. But I found out later that his parents had been putting pressure on him to get married, and he'd found it amusing to introduce *me* as his girlfriend, knowing they would be horrified that he was dating a waitress. That lunch—during which Lord and Lady Sefton could barely bring themselves to speak to me—was one of the most humiliating experiences of my life,' she admitted. 'But not as humiliating as when I overheard Miles assure Lord Sefton that our relationship wasn't serious, and that he was only dating me because he wanted to take me to bed.'

She caught the expression in Raul's eyes and said bitterly, 'I know what you're thinking: why *else* would a member of the landed gentry have dated a waitress? Still, it proved what my mother always said—that all men are selfish and not to be trusted, and certainly not worth wasting your emotions on.'

Suddenly conscious that her raised voice was attracting attention from the other guests waiting to enter the banqueting hall, she took a deep breath, and moments later a footman appeared to escort her and Raul to their table.

'Your mother clearly has strong views on the inadequacies of the male species,' Raul commented dryly when they were both seated. Although perhaps that was not so surprising, he mused, recalling that Libby had told him her father had abandoned her mother before she had even been born.

'Mum had a lot of bad experiences with men.' Libby immediately sprang to Liz's defence. 'They always let her down.'

Including Pietro Carducci, she brooded, anger flaring inside her when she remembered how heartbroken her mother had been when her lover had failed to call her after the cruise. Admittedly Pietro had made provision for Liz and Gino in his will, but it was too late, she thought sadly. Liz had died believing that Pietro had abandoned her just as Libby's father had done.

'I won't make the same mistakes as Mum,' Libby said fiercely. 'Most of the men she dated when I was a child were creeps. I'm *never* going to put Gino through the misery of feeling that he has to compete with a new man in my life.'

Raul frowned. 'What do you mean?'

'I mean that until Gino is eighteen *he* is going to be the only man in my life. Romance is a fool's game anyway, and in my experience highly overrated,' Libby said bleakly, remembering the tears she had wasted over Miles.

'You can't seriously intend to remain single for the next seventeen years?' Raul could not hide his surprise at the vehemence of her tone. 'Wouldn't you like to get married one day? Perhaps have more children so that Gino grows up as part of a family?' He kept his tone deliberately casual while he digested the unwelcome news that Libby did not seem to have marriage on her agenda.

She shook her head. 'It's a nice idea, and I suppose if I'm honest a part of me wants to believe in the fairytale of falling in love with a man who would be a wonderful stepfather to Gino and all of us living happily ever after.

But the reality is that something like one in three marriages end in divorce, and I'd rather concentrate all my energy on Gino than risk a relationship that may not work out.'

She paused, unaware of the wistful expression in her eyes as she added, 'I can't deny that I'd love Gino to have a proper family: a father, brothers and sisters. It was what I wanted more than anything when I was a child. But the fact is that Gino's father is dead. He only has me, and I will do my best to be a mother *and* a father to him.'

The arrival of a waiter to serve the first course put an end to the conversation. Raul sipped his wine and considered what Libby had told him. He was frustrated that she did not fit the image he had formed of her when he'd first realised that she had been Pietro's mistress. He had formed many unpleasant ideas of her, and had never expected her to evoke his sympathy. But now he recalled how Libby had said that when she had told Pietro she was pregnant with his child he had ignored her. She clearly believed that his father had let her down, as her own father had abandoned her mother. She had read in the papers of Pietro's death and must have known that she would have been entitled to a maintenance award for Gino, but instead of contacting the Carducci family she had disappeared and it had taken him months to find her.

The possibility that he might have misjudged Libby tormented Raul's mind throughout the dinner and the interminably long speeches which followed. But sitting beside her, inhaling her delicate perfume while his eyes strayed to the creamy upper slopes of her breasts displayed so tantalisingly above her low-cut dress, proved an even greater torment for his body. Lust was another emotion he had *not* expected to feel for his father's mistress, he thought irritably, shifting his position slightly to ease the uncomfortable sensation of his arousal straining against the zip of his trousers.

Libby was relieved when the after-dinner speeches finally came to an end. She had understood very little about EU trade policies or new business opportunities in China, and as her concentration had wavered she had grown increasingly aware of the man at her side. Raul seemed to have taken his suggestion that they should be friends for Gino's sake to heart, and throughout the meal he had subjected her to the full megawatt force of his charisma. He was a witty and entertain-

ing companion, and every time he smiled she
found it impossible to resist his sexy charm.

'What's happening now?' she asked him as
they stood up from the table and joined the
throng of guests walking out of the banqueting suite.

'Now everyone races towards the bar, desperate for a drink after sitting through two
hours of dull speeches.' Raul glanced down
at her, his eyes glinting with amusement and
a latent sensual heat that made her heart race.
'Can I get you more champagne? Or would
you like to dance?'

Libby glanced around and realised they
were now in a vast ballroom. 'I don't think
I'd better risk any more alcohol after the two
glasses of champagne I had at dinner.' She
caught her breath when Raul slid his arm
around her waist and led her onto the dance
floor.

'Wise choice,' he murmured, lowering
his head so that his warm breath fanned her
cheek. The feel of his lean, hard body pressed
close against her warned Libby that he was
a far greater risk to her equilibrium than another glass of champagne, but she told herself
that she did not want to spoil their tenuous
friendship by pulling out of his arms. 'Relax,'
he bade her, his voice as sensuous as molten

honey, and she could not prevent a quiver of reaction when he traced his fingertips lightly up and down her spine.

She lost all sense of time as they drifted around the ballroom, hip to hip, her breasts crushed against the steel wall of his chest as he imperceptibly tightened his arms around her. Other guests passed them by on the dance floor, but she was only aware of Raul. When he finally loosened his hold and eased away from her the dull ache in her pelvis had intensified to a hot, frantic throb, and she stared at him dazedly when he steered her towards the door.

'It's midnight, and we have a forty minute drive back to the Villa Giulietta,' he informed her gently. 'I assume you would prefer to go back to the villa, so that you are there when Gino wakes tomorrow morning, rather than spend the night at my apartment?'

'Oh, yes—definitely,' Libby agreed quickly, shame sweeping through her when she realised she had not thought about Gino for the past few hours. How *could* she have forgotten him so easily when he had been the most important person in her life for the past ten months? The truth was that Raul dominated her senses. Even now her treacherous body trembled at his closeness as he ushered her across the foyer and out of the hotel.

They were both silent on the journey from Rome. Raul appeared to be lost in his thoughts, and after one glance at his hard profile Libby closed her eyes in a desperate attempt to lessen her awareness of him. Eventually the crunch of the Lamborghini's tyres on the gravel drive told her they had arrived back at the villa, and as she lifted her lashes she could not restrain a gasp at the sight of the vast black lake spread out in front of the house, dappled with silver moonlight and reflecting a myriad diamond stars.

'It's so beautiful,' she whispered in an awed voice.

Too impatient to wait for Raul to walk round and open her door, she jumped out of the car and headed towards the lake. But walking in her high heels on the gravel was almost impossible, and she stepped onto the lawn and kicked off her shoes before running down to the water's edge. The damp grass was cool against the soles of her feet, and the soft breeze from the lake whispered across her skin like a lover's caress. She tipped her head back to stare at the stars and laughed in sheer delight at the beauty of the night.

'I love the way the moonlight casts a silver

path across the black water. It makes you want
to strip off and dive in.' She spun round to
Raul, her face alight with pleasure.

Her boundless enthusiasm was irresistible,
he thought, his mouth curving into a smile.
'I'm all for you stripping off,' he murmured
dulcetly, 'but you may get a shock if you dive
in. The water temperature drops considerably
at night.'

Heat scalded Libby's cheeks. 'I was speaking figuratively,' she mumbled, her heart jerk-
ing unevenly beneath her ribs as Raul walked
towards her, his eyes glinting with sensual
promise. He halted in front of her, so close
that she could feel the heat from his body,
and her breath hitched in her throat when he
slid his hand beneath her chin and tilted her
face to his.

'What a pity,' he murmured, the amusement in his voice fading to be replaced with
a stark hunger. 'There's nothing I would not
do at this moment to see you naked in the
moonlight, *cara*.'

'Raul…' Libby's faint protest drifted away
on the breeze. She had wanted him to kiss
her since he had walked into the hotel bar
earlier and stared at her with undisguised
desire blazing in his eyes. All evening she
had ached for this moment. The chemistry

between them was too overpowering to be denied, and now, as he slowly lowered his head, she trembled with anticipation and a wild, ferocious excitement that exploded in a starburst of pleasure at the first brush of his lips across hers.

Raul wanted to take it slow, to savour the moist softness of Libby's mouth in a leisurely tasting, but his plans were blown sky-high the moment he claimed her lips and felt her instant response. Passion did not simply flare between them, it roared into hot, urgent life, as untamed and out of control as a forest fire, consuming them both. He pulled her into the cradle of his hips and groaned when she moved sinuously against him, his erection so immediate and so shockingly hard that there was no way she could not be aware of it.

Her breasts were crushed against his chest, and he could feel the hard peaks of her nipples through his silk shirt. *Dio*, he had never felt such hunger for a woman. Desire pounded in his veins and demolished his ability to think. His usual cool logic had been replaced with primitive sexual need and he tangled his fingers in her fiery curls and tugged her head back to expose the slender column of her white throat.

Libby could not restrain a little moan of

pleasure when Raul slid his lips down her neck. Every nerve-ending in her body was attuned to the brush of his mouth on her skin, and a tremor ran through her when he trailed hot, hungry kisses along her collarbone and bare shoulder. Held tightly against him, she was unaware that he had slid the zip of her dress down until the strapless bodice suddenly felt loose. Heart thumping, she tried to ease her mouth from his to protest, but he increased the pressure of his lips in a sensual assault that left her dazed with desire, and when he finally lifted his head she did nothing to stop him as he slowly peeled her dress down until her breasts spilled into his hands.

'You are exquisite,' he muttered hoarsely.

His voice was no longer coldly arrogant but rough with need, and Libby's faint spark of resistance melted away as he stroked his thumb-pads across her nipples so that they immediately hardened into tight, tingling peaks. Somehow, without her being aware that they had moved, Raul had guided her beneath the shadow of a tall pine tree, and she leaned back against the trunk, grateful for its support as he lowered his head and closed his lips around one nipple while he continued to roll its twin between his fingers.

The pleasure of his mouth on her breasts was indescribable, and she instinctively arched her back, no thought in her head other than that he should continue to stroke his tongue across each sensitive crest. Nothing in her life had prepared her for this clawing, clamouring need that caused her entire body to throb with desire. She wanted Raul with an instinctive, primitive hunger—wanted to feel his naked skin on hers and to take the solid length of his erection that she could feel jutting into her belly deep inside her.

He tugged up her long skirt until it bunched around her waist, and she trembled with anticipation when he slipped his hand between her thighs, forcing her to part them slightly, before he ran a finger over the lacy panel of her knickers. At the same time he drew one nipple fully into his mouth and suckled her. The sensual tugging sensation sent arrows of pleasure from her breasts to her pelvis. With a little sob she arched her hips towards his hand, and caught her breath when he slid his finger inside her knickers and discovered the slick wetness of her arousal.

She had never allowed a man to touch her so intimately before—not even Miles, whom she had been so sure she had been in love with. This hot, pulsing need that Raul was arousing in her was lust, not love—she knew that—but right then she did not care *what* the feeling was called. She was just desperate for him to assuage the burning ache between her legs. She closed her eyes and let her head fall back, unable to hold back a gasp of wanton delight when Raul ran his thumb-pad very delicately over her clitoris. The effect was instantaneous. Spasms of pleasure ripped through her, causing her muscles to clench; her legs buckled beneath her and she gripped Raul's hair as he cupped her bottom and lifted her, holding her tight against his rock-hard arousal.

'Please...' The spasms were fading, but instinct told her he could give her so much more pleasure.

'What are you asking for, Libby?' His voice was deep and harsh, slicing through the sensual haze that enveloped her. 'Do you want me to take you here and now on the damp grass, in full view of the house?'

Dear God, yes! That was exactly what she wanted. For a few seconds Libby stared at Raul's hard face, all angles and planes in the moonlight, and felt a frantic urge for him to lie her on the ground, strip off her knickers and plunge his swollen shaft into her moist, willing flesh. But the sound of his voice and the cold gleam in his eyes catapulted her back to reality. What was she *doing*? How *could* she have behaved with such wanton eagerness that she had practically begged him to make love to her?

'*Dio!* You said there will be no man in your life while Gino is a child, but clearly you will find it impossible to remain celibate until he is an adult. You are *desperate* for sex,' he taunted savagely. 'But I warn you now: I will not allow you to entertain your lovers at the villa. Gino is not going to grow up with a succession of "uncles".'

Libby shook her head, feeling sick as desire slowly ebbed and shame took its place. 'I don't have any lovers,' she said shakily. 'I've never felt like this before. You…' She closed her eyes to try and blot out the memory of how she had responded to him, and realised that honesty was her only hope of convincing Raul she was not the immoral slut he clearly believed she was. 'You make me feel things I've never felt for any other man,' she admitted huskily.

Raul's self-control wavered at Libby's breathy confession, and the temptation to seize her back in his arms and pull her down onto the grass—to take her hard and fast, as his body was screaming at him to do—almost overwhelmed him. Almost—but not quite. Nostrils flaring with the effort of dragging oxygen into his lungs, he stepped away from her and watched her dispassionately as she dragged the bodice of her dress up to cover her breasts. There was a way he could have everything his heart desired: control of Carducci Cosmetics, *and* this sultry green-eyed witch in his bed. He would be a fool not to seize his chance.

'In that case my proposition is even more tenable,' he said softly.

CHAPTER SIX

'WHAT do you mean?' Libby gave a sudden shiver, her skin quickly cooling now that she was no longer in Raul's arms. 'What proposition?'

He saw the tremor that ran through her and frowned. 'You're cold. Here—put this on.' He shrugged out of his jacket, draped it around her shoulders and caught hold of her hand to lead her firmly across the lawn. 'We'll continue this discussion inside.'

Libby would have preferred not to hold a post-mortem on the shockingly wanton way she had responded to him, but Raul's fingers were gripping hers like a vice and she had no option but to hurry alongside him. She burrowed into the jacket, which was still warm from his body and carried the faint scent of his cologne. She had forgotten to collect her shoes, but when they reached the drive and she picked her way cautiously over the gravel he scooped her into his arms and carried her up to the house.

He strode across the hall and into his study, and set her down on her feet before crossing the room and taking a bottle from the drinks cabinet. 'Would you like a whisky? It will warm you up.'

When she shook her head he poured himself a drink and swallowed the amber liquid down in one gulp. She sensed his fierce tension and stared at him in confusion. 'What proposition?' she asked again.

Raul swung round to face her, his dark eyes unfathomable. Ever since the idea of marrying Libby as a way to claim full control of CC had stolen into his mind he had thought of little else. The arguments for and against such a monumental decision had given him a sleepless night and had tormented him all day, so that he had barely been able to concentrate on the crucial board meeting.

He did not want to marry again. Once had been enough, he thought grimly, remembering his bitter divorce from his first wife. He valued his freedom, and was reluctant to sacrifice it, but he valued Carducci Cosmetics above anything—and there would be compensations to taking Libby as his bride, he acknowledged, as he slid his eyes down from her face to her pale shoulders and then lower still to the soft swell of her breasts revealed by the plunging neckline of her dress. She was so very lovely. Just looking at her evoked a dull ache in his gut, and he realised that he no longer cared that she had been Pietro's mistress; the chemistry between them was too strong to be denied.

And there was another important reason to marry her. Gino needed a father. Libby had stated that she would not bring him up with a succession of 'uncles', but it was unrealistic to expect that she would not have a relationship until the baby was older—and Raul found that he hated the prospect of watching from the sidelines while the little boy called another man Papa.

Libby's big blue-green eyes were locked on him, and he knew she was waiting for him to speak. 'I think we should get married,' he said abruptly.

'*What?*'

She must have misheard him, Libby told herself dazedly. Either that or this was his idea of a stupid joke. Perhaps it was wishful thinking? taunted a little voice in her head. Why had her heart leapt with excitement for the nano-second when she had thought he meant that he wanted to marry her? She wasn't in love with him, she wasn't even sure she liked him very much, and she could not understand why she felt drawn to him.

'I don't understand,' she faltered.

'I want to bring Gino up as my son.' The quiet intensity of his tone told her that this was no joke and that he was deadly serious. 'Let me explain,' he said when she gaped at him. 'When Pietro and Eleanora Carducci adopted me they gave me a life that I could never have imagined when I lived in the orphanage—not just wealth and education, but love, and the stability that comes from growing up with two parents. Gino will never know his real father, but if we marry and I adopt him he will grow up with a mother and father, and hopefully siblings,' he added, his eyes gleaming with a sensual heat that sent a tremor through Libby. 'Make no mistake: what I am suggesting is a real marriage,' he told her. 'I will love Gino as my son—just as Pietro loved me—but I have no blood relatives that I am aware of, and I would like to have children of my own.'

'Then surely it would be better to wait until you fall in love, marry a woman you care for, and *then* have children?' Libby argued. 'Heaven knows, enough couples who marry for love still end up in the divorce courts.

What chance would a marriage between us stand when we don't even particularly *like* each other?'

Raul stared at her speculatively. 'I thought we had agreed to become friends for Gino's sake? And I have to say that tonight I thought we succeeded rather well,' he drawled, watching her face flood with colour when she remembered the feverish passion they had shared down by the lake. 'It is precisely the fact that we are *not* in love, and therefore have no expectations about our relationship, that makes me believe our marriage would work.'

He gave a bitter laugh. 'I have tried a conventional marriage, and paid heavily for my mistake. Three years ago I mistook the sexual attraction I felt for my PA for love. Dana assured me that she shared my desire for a family, and we had a great circus of a wedding. But once we were married she continually found reasons why we should put off trying for a child. She preferred to live in our apartment in Manhattan and party every night, and she complained that she hated the villa and found life here boring.'

Raul's jaw tightened as he recalled how his marriage had imploded.

'The only thing that made Dana truly

happy was spending money—although she resented the hours I spent working to make it. At first I was prepared to fund her hobby, but she was a compulsive shopper, and if I ever suggested that she might like to control her spending she would become hysterical and accuse me of being a tyrant who wanted to keep her barefoot and pregnant. Not that her falling pregnant was ever likely,' he said flatly. 'After a year of increasingly bitter rows it was clear that the marriage was a disaster, and during one of our many screaming matches Dana admitted she had lied about wanting children, and had only married me because I was wealthy enough to give her the extravagant lifestyle she craved. We agreed to divorce and I offered her a generous settlement, including the Manhattan apartment. But that wasn't enough for my dear ex-wife. She wanted every last drop of blood she could squeeze out of me, and even made a claim on the Villa Giulietta.'

'But I thought you said she hated the villa?' Libby said faintly, stunned by the revelation that Raul had once been married. His past relationships were of no interest to her, she reminded herself, so why did she feel so stupidly jealous of his ex-wife?

'Dana knew I would pay whatever she

demanded in return for her agreement to relinquish her rights to the villa. Her divorce settlement made legal history in the American courts—and I learned a very expensive lesson,' Raul said savagely. 'I will never fall for the illusion of love again, but I want Gino to have two parents, as I did when the Carduccis adopted me. You said yourself you longed to have a proper family when you were a child,' he reminded Libby when she stared at him in dumbstruck silence.

'I said I wanted to believe in the fairytale of a happy ever after family, but I'm not sure it really exists.'

'We can make it exist if it's something we both want.'

As Raul spoke he was startled to realise that he no longer only wanted to persuade Libby to marry him so that he could claim full control of the company. Everything he had said to her was true; he wanted to repay his adoptive father for all he had done for him by adopting Pietro's son, and he felt a fierce longing to hold his own child in his arms and finally have a blood link with another human being. Taking full control of CC until Gino was eighteen *was* important to him. But instead of divorcing Libby, as he had planned, he saw no reason why they should not have a successful marriage built on their mutual desire for a family—as well as their physical desire for each other.

Libby shook her head, trying to ignore the voice of her conscience which was whispering that Raul's suggestion made a crazy kind of sense. He was offering to be a father to Gino, and that alone demanded her serious consideration when she had spent her childhood wishing that she had a father.

If she married Raul she would no longer live in fear of him discovering that she was not Gino's mother and banishing her from the villa. But he had said it would be a real marriage. Her eyes were drawn to his hard body, and a quiver ran through her when she remembered how his bold caresses had taken her to such a level of excitement that she had been desperate for him to make love to her properly. Would he be able to tell that not only had she had not given birth to Gino, but that she had never even had sex? Not if she pretended to be experienced, the voice in her head pointed out. But that would be another lie to add to all the others she had spun. Wouldn't it be better to admit the truth about Gino's parentage now?

She chewed on her lip, torn between her guilty conscience and her fear of losing Gino.

Nothing had changed. If she revealed that she was Gino's half-sister and had no legal rights to him Raul would still fight her for custody of the baby—and if he won he might go ahead and adopt Gino, and send her back to England.

'It would never work,' she said abruptly. 'We're too different. Once this chemistry, or attraction, or whatever it is between us died out we would have nothing in common.'

'I'm not sure we are so different,' Raul mused. 'Our childhood experiences have made us appreciate the value of family life. We both think it would be best for Gino to grow up with two parents. Neither of us plans to marry anyone else, and yet we would both like to have children.'

Raul's deep voice was so softly persuasive that Libby found she could not come up with a single argument against his list of reasons why they should marry, and instead she pictured a scene in the future where she was cradling a newborn baby in her arms while Gino, now a toddler, met his little brother or sister for the first time. She could not deny that she would love to have her own baby some day—a little companion for Gino. But marry Raul! She must be mad to actually be contemplating it—mustn't she?

Wrapped up in her thoughts, she was unaware that he had moved closer to her until he lifted his hand and trailed his finger down from her collarbone to the vee between her breasts exposed by her low-cut dress. 'I don't think we need to worry about the chemistry fading, *cara*,' he murmured, his voice suddenly as rich and sensuous as molten chocolate. 'I'm so hungry for you that I'm unbearably tempted to push you down on the sofa and take you right now—and you would let me, Libby. Don't even think of denying it,' he warned her softly, placing his finger across her lips. Do you think I don't see the way your pulse races whenever I am near you? The way your eyes darken with desire and your lips part in readiness for my kiss?'

His mouth was so close to hers that Libby could taste his warm breath. How *could* she deny her desire for him when she was trembling with her need for him to close the gap between them? His tongue explored the shape of her lips before probing between them, pushing insistently into her mouth. Libby strained towards him, her pride discarded in her eagerness for him to kiss her with all the pent-up passion she could sense simmering between them. Her lashes drifted down, her whole being focused on the pleasure of Raul's wickedly inventive tongue.

But the sound of Gino's stark cry jerked her back to reality. Her eyes flew open and she gasped as she whirled away from Raul and stared towards the door, expecting to see Silvana standing there with the baby.

There was no one there. She stared at Raul, eyes wide with panic. 'I heard Gino cry.'

'The baby monitor,' he explained, nodding towards the device plugged into an electrical socket on the wall behind his desk. 'I've had them installed in every room in the house so that we can always be sure to hear him.'

Even in his study, Libby thought in amazement—which must mean that Raul would not mind being disturbed while he worked. 'I see,' she said slowly. 'That was very thoughtful of you.'

Gino's cries grew louder and he began to cough. Libby heard Silvana's voice speaking gently to the baby, but a strong maternal instinct drove her towards the door.

'I must go to him.' She hesitated, her eyes fixed on Raul's face.

'I would be a good father to him,' he said deeply. 'I swear I will care for him and protect him, love him as Pietro loved me.'

'Yes.' She could see the determination

blazing in his eyes, hear it in his voice. 'I believe you would do that for Gino,' she whispered, moved to tears at the depth of emotion in his fierce avowal.

As a little girl she had dreamed that her father would one day find her, and that he would be strong and brave and would fight the monsters that lived under her bed. Didn't Gino need a father to fight his monsters?

But it was not necessary for her to marry Raul. Under the terms of Pietro's will Gino's future was secure, and he would one day inherit half of Carducci Cosmetics and the Villa Giulietta. But what about his emotional security? Didn't she, better than anyone, understand how important it was for a child to have a father? And Gino would need a positive role model to guide him as he grew into adulthood and inherited his share of the Carducci fortune.

'Marry me and allow me to take care of both of you, *cara*.'

Raul's voice was achingly seductive. He could have no idea how beguiling the concept of being cared for sounded after a lifetime of looking after herself, she brooded. She had adored her mum, but Liz had been too young to cope with motherhood, meaning that Libby had had to learn to be independent from an early age. Now she was solely responsible for Gino. How much easier life would be if she could share that responsibility with someone else?

'I don't know what to do,' she admitted helplessly, terrified of the enormity of the decision facing her.

'Yes, you do,' Raul insisted. 'You must do what is best for Gino, and in your heart you know he needs me.'

He was so strong, so self-assured, and after months of worrying about Gino's health and struggling to cope with her grief at Liz's death, Libby felt so tired. 'Maybe you're right,' she said numbly.

'I am.' Raul's voice rang with conviction and a heady feeling of triumph swept through him. Libby need never know that his over-riding reason for suggesting that they should marry was so that he could take full control of Carducci Cosmetics. He had not been lying when he had told her that he wanted to be Gino's father, or that he wanted them to have children together. Once they were married he would do his best to ensure she quickly fell pregnant; that way she would be too busy caring for a toddler and preparing for the arrival of another baby to realise that she no longer had control of Gino's shares in the company.

Raul could see the indecision in Libby's eyes and sensed the battle waging inside her head. He was renowned in the boardroom as a brilliant tactician, and, sensing victory, he deliberately softened his voice. 'It is in your power to give your son the stable family life you longed for when you were a child. Say yes for Gino's sake, *cara*.'

She couldn't do it. She could not marry a man who did not love her. Could she? Libby's eyes snapped open, and after hours of tossing and turning in bed she finally acknowledged that she was never going to fall asleep while Raul's astounding proposal was going round and round in her head.

She had fled from his study last night after telling him that she needed time to think, but in the pearly softness of dawn her emotions were still in turmoil. Wearily, she threw back the sheets and slipped out of bed, crossing to the window that overlooked the lake. The water was silvery-grey in the early-morning light, reflecting here and there the pink clouds above as the sunrise slowly stained the sky.

'You must do what is best for Gino, and in your heart you know he needs me.' Raul's

words haunted her, for she could not deny the truth of them. Gino needed a father. She believed Raul when he had said that he wanted to adopt the little boy and care for him as Pietro had cared for *him*. Did she have the right to deny Gino what she had wanted more than anything when she was a child: a father, and the security of being part of a proper family, living in a proper home?

She had never felt secure when she and Liz had lived in the commune. When they had eventually moved back to England the other kids at school had been envious of her unconventional upbringing, but the reality was that she had never felt as though she belonged anywhere or to anyone. The adults at the commune had for the most part been absorbed in their own lives, and the children had been undisciplined and unruly, with the older ones frequently bullying the younger ones. Libby had learned to be tough to survive, but she did not want the same for Gino. Children needed rules and boundaries as well as love to help them feel safe, and the fact that Gino would one day inherit a fortune meant that it was vital he had people around him he could trust.

She did not need to marry Raul for him to be a father figure to Gino. But he had told her he would like children of his own. He was embittered by his divorce now, but if she turned him down it was conceivable that in the future he would marry someone else and draw Gino into his new family. The idea of Gino having a stepmother made her blanch. What if Raul and his wife wanted to take Gino away on holiday? And what would happen at Christmas? Would she spend it alone, while Gino celebrated the day with Raul and his family?

She hugged her arms around her, trying to marshal her thoughts. Wouldn't it be better to agree to a loveless marriage and give Gino the stable family he deserved? When her mum had died she had vowed to devote herself to him and do what was best for him, and in a moment of calm clarity she accepted that marrying Raul and allowing him to be a father to Gino was indisputably the greatest gift she could give her orphaned baby brother.

Brilliant sunlight slanted across Libby's face and dragged her from sleep. She sat up, disorientated, and stared blankly at the clock, which showed that it was ten o'clock. She remembered now. Having finally made up her mind to accept Raul's proposal she had fallen back into bed, hoping to catch an hour's sleep before Gino stirred. But she had slept for much longer than she had intended. Gino should have had a dose of his antibiotic at seven, along with a bottle of milk and breakfast…

Heart pounding with panic, she jumped up and shot into the adjoining sitting room, stopping dead at the sight of Raul stretched out on the floor, building towers of wooden bricks which Gino delightedly knocked down.

Two sets of dark eyes focused on her: one pair flecked with amber, which lit up as she moved forward, the other pair as black as midnight and gleaming with sensual heat as they trailed over her wild hair and sunflower yellow nightshirt.

'I can't believe I slept so late,' she burst out, hastily dragging her gaze from Raul's mouth. She focused on Gino and was gratified when he greeted her with a beaming smile and crawled over to her with the speed of a missile. 'Hello, baba,' she murmured, her voice aching with love for the baby as she scooped him up and rubbed her cheek over his silky black curls. 'Has he been okay with you? I mean, he's only ever had me to care for him,' she explained, when Raul's eyebrows rose in silent query. 'He was due his next dose of medicine at—'

'Silvana gave it to him when he had his breakfast,' Raul interrupted her. 'The maid said you were fast asleep, so I sat him in his pushchair and took him for a stroll down by the lake.'

'Oh.' Libby stared at him, disconcerted by the idea of Raul taking Gino off without her. 'I hope he was warm enough. It's important to wrap him up while he has his cough.'

'The thermometer on the patio was showing eighteen degrees Celsius at eight o'clock this morning,' Raul informed her dryly. 'As for Gino's respiratory problems—I've made an appointment for him to see a specialist in Rome next week.'

Relief flooded through Libby. 'Thank you. I've been so worried about him,' she admitted. She bit her lip, wondering how to broach the subject of Raul's marriage proposal. Part of her still wondered if she had dreamed the whole thing, and before she could say anything there was a light tap on the door and Silvana appeared.

'I thought Gino might be ready for a nap,' the nanny said with a smile. As if on cue the baby yawned widely.

'I'm sure he is,' Libby agreed, her heart

lurching when Silvana took Gino through to the nursery, leaving her alone with Raul. She tensed as he strolled over to her, every nerve-ending in her body suddenly tingling when he slid his hand beneath her chin and tilted her face.

'Did you sleep well, *cara*?' As he spoke he lightly touched the give-away dark circles beneath her eyes, and Libby shook her head ruefully.

'No.' She did not explain the reason for her disturbed night, but the shadows in her eyes and the way she tugged her bottom lip with her teeth told their own story. An unbidden feeling of tenderness surged through Raul. She was so young, and so fiercely protective of her son, but there was a vulnerability about her that tugged on his heart. He had expected her to jump at the opportunity to marry a billionaire, he admitted wryly. But instead she had clearly been awake all night, debating the best thing to do for Gino.

'Do you doubt that I will love Gino as much as if he were my own flesh and blood?' he said softly.

Libby was drowning in the liquid warmth of his gaze. 'No, I don't doubt that,' she whispered, unable to tear her eyes from his mouth that was so tantalisingly close to hers. She forced herself to concentrate and voice her doubts. 'It's just that we don't know each other. We're practically strangers.'

Raul heard the note of panic in her voice and once again felt the curious sensation that his heart was being squeezed. 'That is something I intend to remedy over the next couple of weeks. I have arranged to work from the villa, so that I can spend some time with you and Gino, and I will only go to Rome when it is absolutely necessary for me to be at the office.'

'I see.' Libby wet her lips, and her heart began to pound when his head moved imperceptibly lower. 'That will be...good.'

The electricity in the atmosphere crackled, searing them both, and Raul could no longer resist the lure of her moist pink lips. 'Let me show you how good it will be between us,' he said hoarsely. 'I do not only want to marry you for Gino's sake. There is something powerful between us—attraction, chemistry, it doesn't matter what you call it—and it was there from the moment we laid eyes on each other. I challenge you to deny you feel it too.'

'I can't,' Libby admitted shakily, but her voice was no more than a fragile breath, lost beneath the hungry pressure of his lips as he caught her to him and brought his mouth down on hers in a kiss that plundered her soul.

She did not even try to resist. This was where she wanted to be, Libby accepted silently as she wound her arms around his neck to mould her body even closer to his. Her lashes drifted down, her senses focused on the slightly abrasive feel of his skin against cheek and the firm, demanding pressure of his mouth moving on hers in a slow tasting before he pushed his tongue between her lips and explored her with a bold eroticism that made her tremble.

When at last he lifted his head she stared at him dazedly, shaken not so much by his passion but by the faint tenderness she glimpsed in his eyes before his expression was hidden by the sweep of his thick black lashes.

'Will you be my wife, Libby, and allow me to be Gino's father?'

She suddenly felt so emotional that for a moment she could not speak. Maybe every woman felt the same way when faced with a marriage proposal, she told herself. But it meant nothing; Raul meant nothing to her, or she to him. The only reason to accept was an orphaned baby boy. She swallowed the lump in her throat and said steadily, 'Yes'.

His smile stole her breath, but to her disappointment he did not kiss her again, or carry her off to bed and make love to her as she had secretly hoped he would.

'I have some calls to make, so I'll leave you to get dressed, *cara*. Meet me on the terrace for lunch, and we can discuss the wedding.'

Two hours later Libby went to the nursery to collect Gino, and discovered that Raul had not wasted any time in announcing their engagement.

Silvana greeted her with a beaming smile. 'May I offer my congratulations, Libby? Signor Carducci told me that the two of you are to be married, and that he intends to adopt the *bambino*. He will be a wonderful father,' she said approvingly. 'I have seen how much he cares for Gino. I hope that you will be very happy.'

'Thank you.' Libby settled Gino on her hip and made her way along the rabbit-warren of corridors to the main part of the house. As she walked down the central staircase she saw Raul's aunt Carmina emerge from the dining room, and her heart sank when the older woman moved purposefully to the bottom of the stairs, clearly in a furious temper.

'You must think you are very clever.' Carmina launched into her attack as soon as Libby reached the bottom stair. 'First Pietro, and now Raul—both seduced by your youthful body and no doubt your expertise between the sheets. I credited Raul with more sense than to get involved with his father's whore,' she spat viciously. 'I can only think he has lost his sanity if he seriously intends to marry you.'

Libby was determined not to show that she was shaken by the vitriol in Carmina's voice, but she instinctively tightened her arms around Gino. 'I didn't seduce anyone,' she defended herself angrily. 'Raul was perfectly sane when he asked me to marry him—and why shouldn't I be his wife? You know nothing about me, and you have no right to make horrible insinuations about my character.'

'You are a cheap tart who deliberately went after my brother-in-law because you knew he was wealthy, and struck lucky when you conceived his child,' Carmina told her with icy contempt. 'Pietro and I…' Her voice quivered slightly. 'We should have been together—and would have been if he hadn't lost his head over *you*.'

Libby frowned. 'But I thought that Pietro's wife—your sister—died ten years ago? Surely if he had felt anything for you he would have told you in all that time?'

She bit her lip, feeling a pang of sympathy for Raul's aunt, who had clearly been in love with Pietro. No wonder Carmina hated her when she believed Libby had been Pietro's mistress. But even if she could reveal the truth Libby doubted Carmina would feel any happier that Pietro had had an affair with her mother.

'I'm sorry,' she murmured, and immediately realised that her apology had only fuelled the other woman's rage.

'You should not be here—you and your illegitimate son. The Villa Giulietta has been owned by the Carducci family for generations, and it will be a tragic day if a common whore becomes its mistress.'

Libby gasped in shock at the other woman's rudeness. 'Look, I realise you're upset, but you have no right to talk to me like that,' she said shakily. 'Raul—'

'Raul keeps his brains in his underpants, and all he is interested in is getting into your knickers. He has had hundreds of women, but he never keeps them for very long,' Carmina said contemptuously. 'Don't get too comfortable here, Ms Maynard, because he will soon grow bored with you—and then he will replace you in his bed.'

Carmina swung round and swept regally across the hall, leaving Libby feeling sick as she stared after her. 'She's a poisonous old bat,' she told Gino, and gave a rueful smile when he grinned at her, happily unaware of the unpleasant scene that had just taken place.

But she could not forget Raul's aunt's comments—particularly the one about how Raul would grow bored with her. The sexual attraction between them was white-hot at the moment, but how long would it last? And what would happen when it died? Would he take a mistress? Perhaps conduct a discreet affair at his apartment in Rome and return to the Villa Giulietta to play happy families when it suited him?

The terrace extended out from one side of the villa and overlooked the lake to one side and a long rectangular swimming pool, set amid a lush green garden, on the other. Tall marble pillars reached up to a roof formed from the entwined stems of ivy, jasmine and climbing roses, which created a fragrant shady bower.

Raul was seated at the table, idly skimming through a newspaper. His hair gleamed like raw silk in the sunlight, and although his designer shades hid his eyes, nothing could detract from the masculine beauty of his sculpted features. Libby was conscious of a molten sensation between her legs as she walked towards him. It was ridiculous to feel possessive of a man who, until a few days ago, she had never even met. But the idea of him making love to another woman was unbearable.

Could physical attraction alone be responsible for the way her heart skittered in her chest when he got to his feet as she approached and welcomed her with a sensual smile that stole her breath? What else could it be? she asked herself irritably. She might have been mad enough to agree to marry him, but it was only so that Gino would grow up with two parents. She would never be so stupid as to fall in love with him.

Gino grinned when he spied Raul, and held out his chubby arms to him, chuckling when Raul swung him high in the air. The bond between man and child was already undeniable. Lauren suddenly felt ridiculously shy, and could not bring herself to meet Raul's gaze. 'It's so beautiful here,' she murmured, looking around at the expertly landscaped garden and the view of the lake beyond.

He nodded in agreement. 'I thought you might like to spend our honeymoon here at the Villa Giulietta, so that you can get to know the house and grounds properly. But of course if you would prefer to go away somewhere I will arrange it.'

Libby gave him a startled glance. 'There's no rush to plan the honeymoon, is there?'

'Certainly there is. We are to be married in two weeks' time. The necessary paperwork is already being taken care of.'

'Two weeks!' Shock caused Libby's voice to rise several octaves. 'That's too soon.'

Raul had strapped Gino into his highchair and the baby was now happily chewing on a rusk. 'I see no reason why we should wait,' he murmured as he moved to stand in front of her.

Her body instantly reacted to his closeness; her breasts felt heavy, and her nipples tightened and pushed against the restriction of her bra. She was embarrassed by the effect he had on her, but she could not prevent her eyes from focusing on his mouth, remembering how he had kissed her earlier and longing for him to do it again.

'We both agree that Gino's needs are paramount. And he needs both of us,' Raul insisted. 'The sooner we marry, the sooner

I can start proceedings to adopt him. Who knows? Maybe his first word will be Papa!'

Emotion washed over Libby. Papa was going to be such an important word in Gino's vocabulary. She knew that marrying Raul was the right thing to do, but she couldn't forget his aunt's assertion that he had had countless mistresses. She stared at his handsome face and felt a sharp stab of jealousy at the thought of all the beautiful women he must have slept with.

'If this is going to work, there will have to be certain ground rules,' she said abruptly.

She flushed when Raul gave her a look of arrogant amusement. 'What kind of rules?'

'Well, fidelity for one. I think we should agree that we will both remain faithful within our marriage. Children are very perceptive, and I don't want Gino to grow up thinking that it's okay for his father to have affairs with other women. You are going to be his most important role model and you should set a good example...' She tailed off, her face scarlet as she wondered if she had revealed too much of herself and her insecurities. 'Your aunt says that you've had hundreds of mistresses, but none of your relationships last long and you'll soon grow bored with me.' The words spilled out in a rush.

Raul frowned. 'When did you speak to Carmina?'

'Oh, we had a run-in just before I came to find you.' Libby grimaced. 'She doesn't like me, and she made it clear that she disapproves of you marrying me.'

Having already been subjected to his aunt's views on his choice of bride, Raul was not surprised by the tremor in Libby's voice. What *did* surprise him was how angry he felt with Carmina, and the surge of protectiveness he felt for Libby. 'I'm sorry if my aunt upset you. She will not do so again,' he promised grimly. 'I will arrange for her to return to her house in Rome immediately. It is a move that is long overdue anyway,' he explained, when she looked worried.

He studied her speculatively for a few moments. 'As to my previous relationships—I am a thirty-six-year old red-bloodied male, and I have not lived like a monk. But I certainly have not had hundreds of lovers.' Libby seemed to have developed a sudden fascination with the marble floor tiles and only reluctantly lifted her head when he cupped her chin and exerted gentle pressure. 'I agree with the fidelity rule. We may not be marrying for conventional reasons, but I am prepared to make a serious commitment to you as well as to Gino.'

It was ridiculous to feel so relieved by his statement, Libby told herself impatiently. And even more ridiculous to feel a little pang of regret because he had underlined the fact that they were marrying for convenience rather than love. She was too old to believe in fairytales, and Raul was not her prince.

He was still holding her chin so that her face was tilted to his. He brought his other hand up and tangled his fingers in her bright silky curls, the expression in his eyes causing her heart to miss a beat. 'I don't think there's a chance I will grow bored with you, *cara*. You are fiery and exciting and no woman has ever turned me on the way you do.' He stared down at her and desire coiled in his gut. 'I'm glad you decided to wear your new clothes,' he murmured. Her dress was a simple sheath of pale blue silk which moulded her breasts and the slight flare of her hips. She looked elegant and at the same time sinfully sexy— and he had never professed to be a saint.

After his disastrous marriage to Dana he had been adamant that he would never marry again, and his desire for full control of CC was the major factor in his decision to marry Libby. But it was not the only factor, he acknowledged as he brushed his lips across hers and felt her instant response. There would be compensations to taking Libby as his wife. Heat surged through his veins when she opened her mouth so that he could slide his tongue into her moist warmth, and he gave in to the temptation to slide his hand over her silky dress and cup one soft breast in his palm. Only the presence of Gino prevented him from pushing her skirt up and taking her on the table, and he was breathing hard when he tore his mouth from hers.

'Two weeks cannot pass quickly enough for either of us, *cara*,' he said thickly, satisfaction surging through him when she stared at him with dazed eyes and ran her tongue over her swollen lips. 'When you have had lunch I will take you to Rome so that you can choose a wedding dress.'

CHAPTER SEVEN

THE following days flew past with frightening speed. The wedding was only to be a small civil ceremony, and as Raul had taken charge of all the arrangements Libby felt strangely detached from it all—while at the same time it loomed on her horizon like a dark and ominous cloud.

'Do you wish to invite any of your family or friends from England to the wedding?' he asked during dinner one evening.

Since his aunt's departure from the villa they had taken to eating on the terrace rather than in the formal dining room. Dinner by candlelight with the view of the lake spread before them was romantic, and Raul was no longer a coldly arrogant stranger but such a charming and attentive companion that Libby looked forward to the evenings when they were alone together.

To her relief he never made any reference

to her supposed affair with Pietro—indeed, he seemed to go out of his way to avoid the subject, and encouraged her to talk about her childhood living in Ibiza.

She turned her head from where she had been staring dreamily at the sun as it sank below the horizon, streaking the indigo sky and the vast expanse of water beneath it with crimson and gold. 'I lost contact with many of my friends when I moved from London to Cornwall,' she explained. 'My closest friend Alice would have come, but she's tied up in a big court case and can't get away.'

Raul was puzzled that she made no mention of her mother, but refrained from asking about her. He knew that Libby had had an unconventional childhood, living in the commune, and in his opinion her mother had been an irresponsible parent. He wondered if Libby had fallen out with her, but decided that it was none of his business.

She seemed to confirm his suspicions when she said cheerfully, 'There'll just be me and Gino on the Maynard side of the church. I hope you don't have hundreds of relatives, because I'll feel totally overawed.'

Beneath her breezy tone Raul heard the loneliness in her voice, and something tugged in his chest. Libby might act tough, but underneath she was achingly vulnerable. Perhaps she had sought a relationship with Pietro, who had been so much older than her, because she had hoped he would give her the security she had never had during her childhood? He brooded, startled by the unexpected surge of protectiveness he felt for her.

He had come to realise that, far from being the gold-digger he had first assumed, she had no interest in money. Indeed, his insistence that she should buy a wedding dress had resulted in a furious row, with Libby arguing that it would be a waste of his money and that she would wear one of the outfits she had bought when she had first arrived in Italy. Eventually, after much bullying, she had reluctantly agreed to choose a dress, but the bill she had presented him with had been small change compared to the forty thousand pounds his first wife's designer wedding gown had cost.

'If you have no close family members who did you appoint as Gino's guardian in the event of your death?' he asked her.

Libby gave him a startled look. 'I didn't. I mean, I'm twenty-two and perfectly healthy...'

'I appreciate that, but nothing in life is one hundred percent certain. I assumed you would have planned for Gino's care?'

It hadn't even occurred to her, Libby thought guiltily. And her oversight was all the more unforgivable when Liz's failure to appoint *her* as Gino's guardian was the very reason she had deceived Raul into thinking that *she* was the little boy's mother. Raul was right: life did not come with a guarantee. Supposing she had been killed in an accident? she thought, feeling sick. Gino would have been left all alone in the world and reliant on Social Services to care for him. The idea was too awful to contemplate, but fortunately she did not have to—because she was going to marry Raul, and he was going to adopt Gino, and whatever happened in the future he would be safe.

Libby clung to that thought a few days later, when she stepped into the dress she had chosen to get married in. It was not remotely bridal, she acknowledged as she twirled in front of the mirror and admired the way the multi-coloured silk skirt, overlaid with layers of chiffon, swirled around her legs. Aware that Raul disapproved of her favourite purple tie-dyed skirt and her penchant for green and orange, preferably worn together, she had planned to buy something elegant and sophisticated in a pastel shade, but the moment she had seen the dress she had fallen in love with its jewel-bright colours.

It was not as if theirs was a conventional marriage—there was no reason why she should wear a conventional wedding dress, she reassured herself. Raul was marrying her for the same reason that she was marrying him—for Gino. In all probability he would not care what she wore.

But despite her bravado her heart was thumping when she walked out of her bedroom for what, she realised shakily, was probably the last time. Her clothes had already been moved to the master bedroom that she would share with Raul, whilst another room further along the first floor corridor had been turned into a new nursery for Gino.

They might not be marrying for conventional reasons, but Raul had insisted that their marriage would be a real one, which meant that tonight he would expect her to join him in his huge bed and then he would—her imagination came to an abrupt halt. She only had a school textbook knowledge of what would happen next, and the realisation that she was going to have to act as if she knew what she was doing weighed heavy on her mind.

She rounded a corner and halted at the top of the great sweeping staircase which led to the marble floored hall below. Raul was there, looking so breathtakingly handsome in a dark, expertly tailored suit and white silk shirt that her heart thudded harder. He was unaware of her presence, and she studied him greedily, noting how his jet-black hair gleamed like raw silk in the sunlight, and how he moved with lithe grace for such a big, powerful man. He was holding Gino, who looked gorgeous in his new blue and white sailor suit, but when the baby squirmed restlessly in his arms he set him on his feet and hunkered down beside him, holding Gino's hands to help him balance.

Walking was Gino's new discovery, and although he could not yet take any steps unaided he loved being on his feet. He gurgled in delight as Raul patiently guided him across the floor, his little face alight with pleasure and trust in the man who was supporting him.

A lump formed in Libby's throat as she watched them. During the past two weeks she had become convinced that Raul would be a fantastic father. Every day he had visited the nursery to play with Gino, and the incongruous sight of him crawling around the floor with the baby, or patiently stacking bricks for him to knock down, had left her deeply impressed. There was genuine affection in his voice when he spoke to the little boy, and Gino patently adored Raul.

She moved to the top of the stairs just as Raul scooped Gino back into his arms, laughing as he said, 'Up you come, *piccolo*, before you wear those little legs out.' He glanced up and fell silent as Libby walked down the stairs, his expression unfathomable as he studied her appearance.

He hated her dress, she thought miserably. Why hadn't she chosen that cream silk suit that had made her look ultra-sophisticated?

'I realise it's probably not what you had in mind,' she burst out when she reached the bottom stair and he still made no comment.

'No,' Raul conceded, wondering what it was about this woman that caused fire to surge through his veins, not to mention other pertinent areas of his body, he thought derisively, supremely conscious of his rock-solid erection. 'But you never fail to surprise me, *cara*.'

'I did try on a cream outfit in the bridal-wear shop, but it just wasn't me,' she told him earnestly. 'I love bright colours.'

'I realise that.' Raul swept his eyes over her, taking in her glorious red curls and the brilliantly coloured dress that moulded her full breasts and emphasised her tiny waist, while the floaty layers of the chiffon skirt drew attention to her slender legs. She was vibrant and intense, and he was climbing the walls with his ferocious need to take her to bed and enjoy the fiery passion she exuded from every pore. 'You look very beautiful,' he said deeply. 'You would not be you without your rainbow colours. And I have to admit that orange and green are growing on me.'

Startled by the serious note beneath his amused comment, Libby's eyes flew to his face, and she felt a curious fluttering feeling inside at the warmth of his gaze. A silent message seemed to pass between them, as elusive as a wisp of smoke. It drifted away before she could grasp it or comprehend it, but the fluttering feeling grew stronger when his mouth curved into a sensual smile.

'I made the mistake of thinking you would wear a conventional wedding dress and so I ordered flowers to match,' he said, taking a bouquet of pure white rosebuds from the

dresser behind him and handing it to her. 'I
hope you like them.'

The arrangement was starkly simple and
yet exquisitely lovely, with the petals of the
mass of rosebuds just beginning to unfurl to
release their delicate perfume. Tears stung
Libby's eyes and she dared not look at Raul
in case he should see them. She had never expected flowers on her wedding day. 'They're
perfect,' she said quietly. 'Thank you.'

His smile widened. 'Come,' he invited,
holding out his hand to her. 'I believe we have
a wedding to attend, Ms Maynard.'

Raul's mobile phone rang as they walked
out of the villa. He frowned, knowing that
it was likely to be a business call, and was
tempted for the first time ever to ignore it. But
the ringing persisted, and when he took his
phone from his jacket he saw that the caller
was his lawyer, Bernardo Orsini.

'I'm sorry, but I need to take this,' he apol-
ogised to Libby as they reached the car where
his driver, Tito, was waiting to take them to
the wedding hall in the nearby town.

'Bernardo?'

'I just wanted to let you know that everything is in place for you to be confirmed as
sole chairman of Carducci Cosmetics once
Elizabeth Maynard is married.' The lawyer

laughed softly. 'I assume that *is* the reason for your hasty trip down the aisle? I congratulate you, Raul, for acting so swiftly. I presume you will allow a suitable amount of time to pass before you file for divorce? I hope the duration of your marriage will not be too disagreeable.'

Raul watched Libby as she bent over to strap Gino into his baby seat in the back of the car and felt an uncomfortable tightening in his groin as he studied the rounded curves of her bottom, moulded so enticingly beneath her silk dress. 'I'm sure I'll survive,' he assured the lawyer dryly.

But as he climbed into the car beside her and inhaled the delicate, floral fragrance of her perfume he was shocked to realise that his desire for control of CC had not been uppermost in his mind for days. It was his desire for Libby which dominated his thoughts.

The day passed in a blur, leaving Libby with a kaleidoscope of images that she knew would remain with her for ever. First there had been the ornate wedding hall in a beautiful *palazzo* overlooking Lake Bracciano, where she and Raul had made their vows. The ceremony had been witnessed by Tito and Silvana—who had somehow persuaded Gino to sit quietly on her lap—and Raul's close friends Romano and Flaviana Vincenti. Libby had met the couple and their two cherubic little daughters a few days before the wedding, and assumed Raul had told them that he was marrying her so that he could be Gino's father. But to her surprise they clearly believed that it was a love match.

'We never thought Raul would marry again after what he went through with Dana,' Flaviana said at the end of the ceremony, when she kissed Libby's cheek and offered her congratulations to the newlyweds. 'You must be very special to have stolen his heart.'

'Oh… But…' Libby was prevented from replying when Raul's dark head swooped and he claimed her mouth in a long, fiercely passionate kiss that left her dazed and hot-cheeked. When he finally released her she realised that a photographer had been busily snapping them.

'The reason for our marriage is a private matter between us,' he murmured as they filed out of the wedding hall. 'Flaviana is an incurable romantic, and I see no reason to shatter her illusions.'

And that, presumably, was the reason why Raul was so attentive throughout the wedding reception: a celebratory dinner at a charming little restaurant, followed by a cruise along the lake, during which the adults drank pink champagne and the Vincentis' little daughters ran excitedly up and down the boat, much to Gino's entertainment.

It had been an unexpectedly beautiful day, Libby mused as she crept out of the nursery after checking on Gino later that night. She stood in the doorway and listened to the regular sound of his breathing for a few moments, relieved that he no longer made the horrible rasping noise in his chest. A few days ago she and Raul had taken him to see a top specialist, who had given him a thorough check-over, sent him for X-rays, and finally assured them that the pneumonia had not caused permanent damage to his lungs.

'You have a fine son, and I am confident he will grow up to be a strong, healthy boy,' the doctor had said with a smile as he handed the baby back to Raul.

As soon as the adoption process was complete Gino would have a father and would grow up with the love and security of two parents, Libby thought as she walked down the corridor towards the master bedroom. It was what she wanted—the reason why she had married Raul. But now their wedding day was over and their wedding night was about to begin. She felt sick with nerves, yet at the same time she was conscious of a frisson of anticipation at the thought of Raul making love to her.

The chemistry between them was almost tangible; every time they were in the same room she was aware of the simmering sexual tension that made his eyes darken and evoked a restless ache deep within her. Her fear was not so much of losing her virginity, but the knowledge that she must fool him into believing that she had had sex before.

Perhaps she should tell him the truth? Her steps slowed and she gnawed on her bottom lip. Wouldn't honesty be the best policy now that she and Raul were married? Surely he would understand why she had pretended to be Gino's mother if she explained her fears that he might be taken away from her?

But what if Raul *didn't* understand? What if he was so angry at her deception that he had their marriage annulled, claimed custody of Gino, and banished her from the Villa Giulietta? The gamble was too great, she decided. She was not prepared to risk losing Gino, and so her secret must remain. Tonight she must play the part of sensual seductress and convince Raul that she was sexually experienced.

She pushed open the bedroom door. The bedside lamps had been switched on and the crisp white sheets turned back, but the room was empty. Grateful for the reprieve, she stepped out onto the balcony and took a shaky breath of the scented night air. The velvet darkness pressed around her, with stars shimmering like diamonds in the inky sky and the moon casting its silver gleam across the black waters of the lake.

'To me, this is the most beautiful view on earth.' Raul's deep voice broke the silence, and Libby stiffened when he came up behind her and slid his arms around her waist, drawing her against his chest so that she was conscious of the warmth of his body and the steady thud of his heart.

'The…the lake is especially lovely in the moonlight,' she agreed, her own heart thumping so hard that her voice emerged as a whisper of sound.

'I was not referring to the lake, *cara*.'

Hot, pulsing need coiled in Raul's gut as he pushed Libby's fiery curls aside and pressed his mouth to her slender white neck. He had wanted her the moment he had set eyes on her, and even the shocking discovery that

she had been Pietro's mistress had not less-
ened his desire. He refused to dwell on the
image in his head of her and Pietro together.
She was his wife now, and he would make
her forget all her previous lovers, he vowed
fiercely, feeling the tremor that ran through
her when he slid the zip of her dress down
her spine.

Libby could hear the blood pounding in her
ears, and trepidation and a fierce excitement
corkscrewed through her when Raul pushed
her dress over her shoulders and drew it lower
and lower, until he had bared her breasts. She
swallowed when he cupped each soft mound
in his palms, and could not restrain a little
gasp as he took her nipples between his fingers and tugged gently, so that they swelled
and hardened into tight, aching peaks.

'Please...' The pleasure was indescribable.
Arrows of sensation shot from her breasts to
her pelvis and molten heat flooded between
her legs, her arousal so swift and so shockingly intense that her nervousness was swept
away by a tidal wave of need for him to touch
her where she ached to be touched.

'You are so responsive, *cara*, and your eagerness is such a turn on,' Raul said thickly
as he spun her round and lowered his head
to capture her mouth in a hot, hungry kiss,

sliding his tongue between her lips and exploring her with such erotic skill that Libby's legs buckled and she clung to his shoulders for support. 'I will please you; do not doubt it. I have never wanted any woman the way I want you,' he admitted harshly. 'The chemistry between us is too powerful to deny any longer.'

He swept her up into his arms and in a few strides had carried her from the balcony to the bed, scorching desire in his eyes as he dropped her onto the mattress and quickly removed her dress and shoes. His hand rested lightly on her stomach, and Libby caught her breath when he trailed his fingers down and hooked them in the waistband of her knickers. This was the first time any man had seen her naked, and she suddenly felt acutely vulnerable, her nervousness flooding back when she faced the fact that she was about to give her virginity to a man who believed she was sexually experienced. She had convinced herself that she could hide her innocence, but as he drew her knickers down her legs she instinctively tried to cover herself with her hands, her heart beating like a trapped bird in her chest.

Raul laughed softly. 'I see your red hair is natural,' he murmured. 'Don't hide yourself from me. Open your legs, *cara*. I want to look at you as I touch you. Do you enjoy oral sex?'

He watched her cheeks flood with colour, and was puzzled by the shocked expression in her eyes. She responded with such wild fervour when he kissed her that he had expected her to be impatient for sex. Instead she suddenly seemed shy and uncertain, and he was frustrated that she had made no attempt to touch *him*.

'I...I don't know,' she stammered in a panicky voice.

'Really? You've never...?' He couldn't hide his surprise—but nor could he deny a feeling of satisfaction that he would give her an experience she had never enjoyed with any of her previous lovers. 'Oh, *cara mia*, we must do something about that.'

Libby jerked as if she had been stung when Raul slipped his hand between her thighs. He frowned, and she forced herself to relax so that he would not guess that this was all new to her. Heart hammering, she spread her legs a little, and bit her lip when he pushed them further apart and ran his finger up and down the outer lips of her vagina in a butterfly caress that sent a quiver of pleasure through her. Heat unfurled inside her and built in intensity until she felt the wetness of her arousal flood between her legs. Nothing had prepared her for the exquisite delight of him gently parting her and sliding his finger a little way into her, and she moaned softly when he brushed his thumb pad lightly over the sensitive nub of her clitoris.

It was good—better than good—amazing. Her limbs felt heavy, and she put up no resistance when he pushed her legs wider apart. She sank deeper into the mattress and closed her eyes, so that she could focus on the new and wondrous sensations that Raul was creating with his deft fingers.

The feel of his warm breath fanning the tight cluster of curls at the junction of her thighs caused her lashes to fly open. Surely he wasn't really going to…?

She made a choked sound when he buried his head between her legs and replaced his finger with his tongue. 'No!' Mortified by the shocking intimacy of what he was doing, she caught hold of his hair and tried to pull his head up, but the sensual probing of his tongue was so amazingly good that her resistance melted away and she arched her hips, offering herself up to him and giving little yelps of incredulous pleasure.

A desperate yearning was building deep

in her pelvis—a hot, achy feeling that she knew instinctively only Raul could assuage. Far from wanting him to stop, she was now frantic for him to continue his erotic caresses, and she muttered her protest when he moved and the heat of his mouth was replaced with cool air on her thighs.

'I know; I'm as hungry as you,' Raul growled as he stood up and began to strip out of his clothes.

He would have liked Libby to undress him, but he was so turned-on that it was doubtful he could have withstood her stroking her hands over his body. His trousers joined his shirt on the floor, and he saw her stare at the burgeoning length of his arousal straining beneath his boxers. He did not know why she felt it necessary to maintain the act of *ingénue* after she had responded with such eager enthusiasm to his foreplay. It was likely she'd had dozens of lovers. But he was hardly a saint himself, and he did not want to bed a timid virgin.

It was time he showed her what he *did* want, he decided, amused at the way her eyes widened with apparent shock when he stepped out of his boxers. His massive erection was not surprising when he was about to turn the fantasy of making love to her into reality, but he was burning up with frustration, and this first time was not going to be a leisurely sex session, he already knew. Desire jack-knifed through him as he nudged her legs wider apart and positioned himself over her.

Libby had watched, dry-mouthed, as Raul had undressed, blown away by the masculine beauty of his muscular chest with its covering of fine dark hairs that arrowed down over his abdomen. But when he had stripped off his boxers admiration had turned to astonishment at the awesome size of his arousal. There was no way she was going to be able to take him inside her, she thought fearfully.

Her heart jerked painfully beneath her ribs when he came down on top of her. The feel of his hard body pressing into the softness of hers was alien and frankly terrifying, and a strong instinct for self-protection caused her to tense beneath him. Panic-stricken, she brought her hands up to his chest to push him off her, but he laughed softly as he caught hold of her wrists and forced them above her head.

'I apologise if you find the missionary position boring, *cara*,' he muttered hoarsely, 'but I'm so hungry for you that I'm in danger of coming right now. We have all night to experiment,' he promised.

His words sounded more like a threat to Libby, but as she twisted and squirmed urgently beneath him Raul lowered his head to her breast and drew her nipple into his mouth, sucking and tugging on the taut peak so that sharp arrows of pleasure shot down to her pelvis. 'I love your impatience,' he groaned, mistaking the frantic bucking of her hips as an invitation.

Libby caught her breath when he moved his hand down and unerringly found the slick wetness of her womanhood. The feel of him touching her there, rubbing his thumb over her clitoris, drowned her fears in a swirling mass of sensations. He was driving her towards some magical place she could sense but could not reach, and she felt excitement rather than fear when he withdrew his finger and rubbed the tip of his thick, swollen penis against her.

He eased slowly into her and she let out a shaky sigh of relief. It was all right. It didn't hurt. The feeling of being stretched was strange but not unpleasant, and she relaxed, reassured that he would never know it was her first time. He lifted his mouth from her breast and stared into her eyes, the sinews in his powerful shoulders standing out as he supported his weight and remained poised above her.

'It has to be now,' he said harshly, and gripped her hips to hold her still as he drove into her with a powerful thrust.

His groan of pleasure was cut short when she gave a sharp cry of pain.

Raul stilled, paralysed with shock. *Dio!* It was impossible! He must have imagined the sensation of pushing through a fragile barrier. But she felt so tight around him. Heart pumping as if he had run a marathon, he drew back a fraction, stunned and uncomprehending when he saw that Libby was holding her knuckles against her mouth. Her eyes were dilated with shock. But she could *not* be a virgin, his brain pointed out, the idea was inconceivable.

He moved to withdraw from her, but her vaginal muscles gripped him in a velvet embrace. His blood was pounding through his veins, hot and insistent, and his desire was a pagan, primitive urge that was beyond his power to control. He gritted his teeth, the cords on his neck standing out with the effort of trying to fight it. But he could not hold back—could not prevent himself from sinking deeper into her hot, tight embrace. He

let out a savage groan as the tidal wave overwhelmed him and he pumped his seed into
her in a spectacular release that racked his
body with exquisite aftershocks of pleasure.

CHAPTER EIGHT

LIBBY lay beneath Raul, frozen with shock. Her limbs trembled uncontrollably as reaction set in and she felt horribly sick. She pushed frantically against his chest, desperate for him to release her so that she could escape to the bathroom. His body was heavy on hers, his breathing fast and ragged. He rolled off her and snatched oxygen into his lungs. She could sense his stunned disbelief, and when he turned his head his eyes were as dark and fathomless as the lake on a moonless night.

'What the hell—?' He swore savagely in his native tongue.

Libby could not understand the words, but his meaning was clear. Undoubtedly he wanted an explanation, but she was in no fit state for a post-mortem, and as he reached out to capture her wrist she dived off the bed.

There was blood on the sheet. He stared at the small betraying patch, and then speared her with a savage glance. With a gasp Libby raced into the *en suite* bathroom, flung the door shut and locked it before she staggered over to the toilet and threw up.

Oh, God, what had she done? Even if she hadn't cried out like that when Raul had surged into her, the bloodstained sheet was tangible evidence that she had never given birth to a child.

She hadn't expected it to hurt so much. But, more than that, she thought numbly, she hadn't expected that giving her virginity to Raul would be such an intensely emotional experience. Libby sank weakly against the wall and buried her face in her hands. At the moment when Raul had joined their bodies as one it had hit her with the force of a lightning bolt that she wanted him to love her—as she loved him.

The words went round and round in her head. *She had fallen in love with him.* She couldn't say when exactly it had happened, but she had been drawn to him from the very start, she acknowledged wearily.

Oh, she'd fought him and stood up to him, and told herself she hated his arrogance and didn't care that he despised her for being, as he thought, his father's gold-digger mistress. But beneath her bravado, and despite the huge differences in their upbringing and lifestyles, she had been unable to dismiss the feeling that he was her soul-mate, and that they were somehow linked together by a higher force.

It had not only been his obvious affection for Gino that had prompted her to accept his marriage proposal. Yes, she had wanted him to adopt Gino, so that the little boy would have a father, but the truth was she had hoped that, in the tradition of the best fairytales, Raul would suddenly realise that she was the love of his life.

But when he had thrust into her so forcefully the pain in her heart had been a thousand times worse than the burning sensation caused when he had ripped the delicate membrane of her virginity. She had longed for him to whisper tender words of reassurance, but of course he hadn't. For Raul it had just been sex—and now, thanks to her stupid, melodramatic behaviour, he knew that she wasn't Gino's mother.

She flinched at the sound of hammering on the door and remained sitting on the cold marble floor, hugging her knees to her chest in an instinctively protective gesture.

'*Libby!* Open this damn door before I break it down.'

When she made no response Raul pounded

on the door again until it rattled in its frame. She did not only have to worry about him smashing through the wood, but waking the whole house up. And she could not stay locked in the bathroom for ever. Taking a shaky breath, she forced herself to her feet and wrapped a towel around her shivering body. Her nipples looked starkly pink against her white breasts. They felt ultra-sensitive after Raul had lashed them with his tongue, and she was still conscious of a faint stinging sensation down below, but neither was as painful as the uneven thud of her heart as she unlocked the door.

He had pulled on his trousers but his chest was bare, and Libby felt a ridiculous urge to press her cheek against the whorls of dark hair that covered his gleaming golden skin, and listen to the steady thud of his heart.

Raul was glaring at her as if he would like to throttle her. 'Who is Gino's mother?' he thundered.

She bit her lip and tasted blood. 'Elizabeth Maynard.'

'Don't lie to me!' He fired the words at her like bullets from a gun, his eyes blazing. 'I saw your passport. *You* are Elizabeth Maynard—a very virginal Elizabeth Maynard. Or at least you were until five minutes ago,' he growled harshly. 'You stupid little fool. Why didn't you tell me it was your first time? I would have—' He broke off and raked his hand through his hair, still barely able to comprehend what he had discovered far too late.

In his mind he heard again the thin animal cry of pain she had emitted when he had taken her, and guilt surged through him that he hadn't stopped. His body had betrayed him, he acknowledged bitterly. So greedy for the satisfaction it craved that instead of withdrawing from her he had thrust deeper and to his astonishment come instantly. It had never happened to him before. He prided himself on being a generous lover, and he had never before taken his pleasure with such selfish disregard for his partner. But then he did not make a habit of deflowering virgins, he thought grimly. He felt ashamed and somehow unmanned, and he buried both emotions beneath a torrent of anger.

'I would have taken more care,' he gritted as he stared at her chalk-white face which contrasted so starkly with her golden freckles.

Her eyes seemed too big for her face, and the betraying quiver of her lower lip evoked a curious pain in his chest—like a hand squeezing his heart. His jaw tightened and he dismissed the urge to pull her into his arms. 'Who *are* you?' he demanded savagely.

'I *am* Elizabeth Maynard.' Libby took a deep breath. 'And so was my mother. Mum met your father on the cruise ship and they had an affair. Gino is my half-brother,' she revealed quietly.

'*Your mother* was Pietro's mistress!' Raul swore again, unable to control the emotions storming through him. 'Then where the hell *is* she? Why did you go through the charade of pretending that Gino is your son?'

Libby's grief was still raw, and now it pierced her like an arrow through the heart. 'She's dead,' she said thickly, forcing the words past the constriction in her throat.

Raul stared sharply at Libby's white face, and despite his fury something stirred inside him when he saw the shimmer of tears in her eyes. 'I'm sorry,' he said tightly. 'Were the two of you close?'

'We were more like sisters,' she whispered. 'I miss her every day. For my whole childhood it was just me and Mum, you see. I have no idea who my father is because she didn't like to talk about him. All I know is that he broke her heart. He was married, but Mum hadn't known about his wife. When she told him she was pregnant with me he offered to pay for an abortion.'

She let out a shaky breath. 'Mum couldn't believe it when she found out she was pregnant with Pietro's baby, and when it seemed that he wanted nothing to do with her she felt that history was repeating itself and she had been abandoned by a lover again. But she adored Gino, and she was determined to give him the best childhood she could. That's why she decided to move to Cornwall; she thought it would be a better environment for him than the rough area of London where we lived.

'Then Mum collapsed suddenly and died from a blood clot on her lung,' Libby explained huskily. 'She hadn't made a will, and because she hadn't stipulated that I should have custody of Gino I was scared Social Services would take him.' She darted a glance at Raul's face, but his expression was unreadable. She continued in a rush. 'So I pretended that he was my baby. I love him,' she whispered brokenly. 'He's all I've got—my only link with Mum—and he belongs with me. I know I should have told you the truth…'

'*Per Dio!* You say that now,' Raul flung at her bitterly. 'You lied to me and deceived me…'

'*I had to.*' Libby stared at him desperately,

willing him to understand. 'Pietro stated in his will that he wished for Gino and his mother to live here at the Villa Giulietta. I was afraid that if you knew I wasn't his mother you would fight for custody of him and take him from me—and I couldn't bear that.' Her voice trembled and she forced back the tears that burned her throat, wishing that Raul would stop looking at her with such bitter fury in his eyes. 'You said that Gino needs both of us,' she reminded him huskily. 'That's still true. Liz—my mum—died when he was only a few months old, and I am the only mother he has ever known.'

'But you are *not* his mother,' Raul bit out savagely. Anger burned in his gut. He could not bear to look at Libby now that he knew she was a calculating liar—just as Dana had been.

He jerked away from her and strode across the bedroom and out onto the balcony. He did not know what to say, what to think. Learning that his adoptive father had had a child had been the biggest shock of his life, or so he had thought. But the discovery that the woman he had believed was Gino's mother was a virgin was so astounding that he was still struggling to accept the truth.

One thought stood out from the mass of

emotions swirling in his head, and black rage choked him. It had not been necessary for him to marry her. Libby was not Gino's mother, which meant she had never been entitled to control the fifty percent share of Carducci Cosmetics that Pietro had left in trust for his baby son. If it had been known that Gino's mother was dead, control of the baby's shares would automatically have passed to *him*, Raul thought furiously, and he would not have needed to make Libby his wife in order to take full control of the company.

He sensed her behind him, and jerked his head round to find that she had joined him on the balcony. She had exchanged the towel for her robe. Not the elegant grey silk robe he had bought her, he noted, but the pink fluffy dressing gown she had brought with her from England that make her resemble a marshmallow. Her fiery curls tumbled around her shoulders and Raul thought how young she looked, and how innocent. But she was not quite so innocent now, he brooded grimly, remembering again her cry of pain when he had taken her virginity. For a moment his anger was overshadowed by guilt at the brutal way he had made love to her.

'You should have told me the truth,' he said tautly.

'If I had, you would have taken Gino from me. Wouldn't you?' Libby accused him shakily.

'Of course I damn well would.' He could not deny it. He would have claimed custody of his father's son and become sole chairman of CC until Gino was eighteen without the need for this farcical marriage. 'The hovel you lived in was no place to bring up a child. And what sort of upbringing would he have had with a lap-dancer?'

'I was *not* a lap-dancer—that was my mother,' Libby admitted in a low tone. She saw the look of disdain in Raul's eyes and her temper flared. 'Before you say another word, let me tell you something about Liz. It's true she worked in a grotty men's club, but she had no one to help her or support her, and she refused to live on benefits. I may not have had a conventional upbringing, but I never doubted that she loved me. She was heartbroken when Pietro didn't get in touch after the cruise. Not because she was after his money—she didn't even know he was head of Carducci Cosmetics when she met him—but because she really loved him, and he told her that he had fallen in love with her.'

Libby paused, her throat aching with tears. 'The truth is your father abandoned my mother. But despite that she adored Gino. She would have devoted her life to him, but her life was cut cruelly short…and so I took her place,' she said thickly.

Raul glared at her in frustration. She sounded so damned plausible, but he refused to be taken in by her now he knew how she had deceived him.

'Pietro suffered a stroke two days after he returned home from the cruise,' he said flatly. 'It was the first indication that he had a brain tumour, and it left him paralysed down one side of his body and affected his ability to speak. He was the most honourable, *honest* man I have ever known, and if he told your mother that he loved her then I am certain it was true. But perhaps he felt that she would be better off without him,' he said quietly. 'He did not know then that she was carrying his child, and he was ill and disabled. I'm sure he believed it was fairer to allow your mother to keep her memories of the happy time they had spent together rather than see him as a sick and dying man.'

Libby gripped the balcony rail and willed the tears that blurred her vision not to fall. She did not want to break down in front of Raul. 'It's a terrible tragedy that Gino lost both his parents without ever knowing them.

Mum loved your father, and I know she would have cared for him during his illness,' she said thickly. 'She was a very caring person.'

The raw emotion in her voice caused a curious ache in Raul's chest, but he hardened his heart against her. She had proved that he could not trust her, and he reminded himself that her motives for pretending to be Gino's mother were questionable.

'What about you, Libby? Are you also a *caring person*?' he queried sardonically. 'Is that really the only reason you kept up the charade that Gino was your child?'

'Of course it is.' She stared at him in confusion. 'What other reason could there have been?'

Raul shrugged. His face looked as though it had been carved from marble: so beautiful, but so cold and hard. She wondered what had happened to the man who had smiled at her with such warmth when they had made their wedding vows, and whether he had been a figment of her imagination.

'I think you decided to fool me into believing you were Gino's mother because you knew you would be able to live a life of luxury at the Villa Giulietta. You used Gino as your meal-ticket.'

'No.' She shook her head fiercely, horrified by his accusation.

'Yes, he insisted grimly. 'But you knew you only had the right to live here while Gino was growing up. No wonder you jumped at my suggestion that we should marry. As my wife you would be financially secure for life.'

'That's not true,' Libby denied urgently. 'I didn't have any ulterior motive for accepting your proposal—any more than you did for marrying me. We both did it for Gino's sake, so that he would grow up with two parents.'

Raul speared her with a look of savage contempt. 'Do you really expect me to believe that the lure of money had nothing to do with your decision? You were presented with the opportunity to marry a billionaire and you seized it.'

He ignored the look of hurt in her eyes and pushed past her, unable to bear breathing the same air as her. History had a funny way of repeating itself, he thought bitterly. It was a pity he didn't feel like laughing. He had a reputation as a ruthless adversary in the boardroom, so how had he allowed himself to be taken in by a gold-digger—not once, but twice? Dana and Libby were two of a kind, and he was the biggest fool on the planet.

He pulled on his shirt and turned to find

Libby watching him, her eyes huge in her white face. 'I thought my first marriage was short when it ended after a year, but twelve hours must be a record,' he said brutally.

Libby hugged her arms around herself, shivering despite the warmth of the night, and stared at Raul's hard face. 'Wh…what do you mean? And where are you going?' she asked shakily when he strode over to the door and pulled it open.

'I mean that I will see you in court when I divorce you, *cara*.' The sarcasm in the endearment made her shrivel. 'As to where I am going—hell seems pretty inviting at the moment, compared to being in the same room as you.'

Panic swept through Libby and she shook her head desperately. 'No, you can't mean that—you can't want a divorce. What about Gino? We married for him, remember? To give him a stable childhood…'

'And that is exactly what I intend to give him. It will be better for him if I bring him up on my own than with a callous liar like *you* as his mother. There's not a court in the land that would award you custody of him after the stunt you've pulled,' Raul told her savagely.

Libby gasped and closed her eyes for a few

seconds, willing the room to stop swaying. He couldn't mean it. Her mind whispered the reassurance over and over, but the cold fury in his eyes warned her that he would never forgive her for deceiving him. She needed to make him understand how much she loved Gino, and that everything she had done had been for the baby's sake. But he was walking out of the door. She took a jerky step forward and stretched out her hand. He *couldn't* leave her.

'Raul...please...'

He gave her one last bitter look that ripped her heart in two, and slammed the door before she could reach him. She stood trembling, willing him to walk back in, but the sound of his footsteps along the corridor told her he had gone. Suddenly the dam burst and she crumpled to her knees, tears coursing down her face. This was her wedding night, but thanks to her stupidity the honeymoon was over before their marriage had even begun.

Raul walked swiftly through the silent house and out of the front door, his feet automatically taking him to the place he always went when he needed to be alone. The lake gleamed silver in the moonlight, reflecting the dark shadows of the trees that lined the shore. An owl hooted somewhere, and his footfall thudded on the wooden jetty. It took him mere seconds to untie the mooring rope that secured his sailing boat and he leapt on board and cast off.

A breeze rippled the surface of the water and sent the boat scudding across the little waves. He focused on adjusting the rigging and headed far out onto the lake, the gentle flap of the sail and the lap of the water against the hull soothing his ragged emotions.

Libby was not Gino's mother. She had deceived him and made a fool of him. His nostrils flared as he sought to control his anger, and he sailed on through the velvet darkness, his way lit by the moon and the myriad stars that studded the heavens.

She had done it for money, of course. She had lied to him just as Dana had lied when she had assured him that she wanted children. Dana had been an avaricious bitch who had married him to get her hands on the Carducci fortune, and Libby was no better.

But that was not quite true, he brooded. Libby had shown none of his ex-wife's tendencies to max out his credit card or fill her days shopping for more clothes to cram into her overcrowded wardrobes. Nor had she shown any enthusiasm to visit nightclubs when he had suggested it on the two occasions before their wedding when they had stayed at his apartment in Rome. She would prefer to be at the villa with Gino, she had assured him.

Her dedication to the baby was indisputable; her love for him was absolutely genuine—Raul was convinced of that. He frowned as he recalled the grim, damp flat in Cornwall where he had found her. She must have made huge sacrifices—both materially and personally—for her little half-brother. He was under no illusions about the difficulties she must have faced as a single mother, trying to work and keep a roof over their heads while she cared for the baby. She was a beautiful young woman who should have been able to enjoy all the things that her peers took for granted: fashionable clothes, parties, socialising with friends—dating. But she had given all that up for Gino.

Could any woman love a child who was not her own with such generosity of spirit? he wondered sceptically. Dana would certainly not have done. But he knew of one woman who had. His adoptive mother had taken a feral, emotionally damaged seven-year-old boy into her home, and into her heart. Eleanora Carducci had loved him unconditionally, and he had adored her. But after his acrimonious divorce from Dana he had cynically assumed that all women had a hidden agenda. When he had discovered how Libby had tricked him his first reaction had been utter fury, but now his anger was cooling and he wondered if he had judged her too harshly.

'I didn't have any ulterior motive for accepting your proposal—any more than you did for marrying me. We both did it for Gino's sake.'

Her words hammered in Raul's brain, and guilt reared its ugly head—because he *had* had an ulterior motive, he acknowledged uncomfortably. He had married her to gain control of Carducci Cosmetics, and in truth had been just as guilty of deceit because he had not made her aware of that clause in Pietro's will.

Another thought slipped insidiously into his head. Libby had not been Pietro's mistress. She and his father had never slept together—in fact he had irrefutable proof that she had never given herself to any other man but him. For some inexplicable reason that fact filled him with a heady sense of triumph. He had always thought of himself as a modern guy, and he had absolutely no problem with a woman's right to enjoy a varied sex life with a number of partners—but Libby was his, and he was shocked by the primitive feeling of possessiveness that swept through him, the feeling that he wanted to keep her locked up in the high tower of the villa, away from the gaze of any other man.

There was a glimmer of pale light in the sky when at last he headed back to shore, feeling calmer and in control of his emotions once more, but still unable to answer the question of what the hell he was going to do now.

Shock jolted through him when he caught sight of a figure standing on the jetty. The fiery red hair was instantly recognizable, and as he took the boat closer he saw Libby was wearing jeans and a soft, silvery grey sweater. She looked very young and achingly vulnerable, and he felt a gentle tug on his heart.

'Catch this, will you?' he called to her, and threw a rope onto the jetty. After a moment's hesitation she picked it up. 'Tie it around that post,' he instructed as he brought the boat alongside and jumped out. She surveyed him warily, and he saw that her eyes were red-rimmed, her face so pale that she looked as ethereal as a ghost.

He glanced at his watch. 'It's four a.m. I wasn't expecting you to be up.'

She shrugged, and said dully, 'I haven't slept.'

Her tension was tangible, reminding him of a nervous colt poised to bolt if he came too close. But that was hardly surprising after he had subjected her to the full force of his hot temper.

She looked past him to the soft mist that was drifting across the lake. 'It must be so peaceful out on the water as the sun rises,' she murmured wistfully.

'To my mind it's the closest place to heaven.' He paused, and then said quietly, 'Maybe I'll take you with me some time.'

Her eyes flew to his face and her voice shook as she said desperately, 'Please don't send me away from Gino. I love him, and he loves me. It would be too cruel...'

'I know.' He exhaled heavily. 'I am not an ogre. I am fully aware of your devotion to him, and that in his eyes you are his mother.'

For the first time since he had slammed out of the bedroom Libby felt the terrible tension that gripped her muscles ease a little. 'I know what I did was unforgivable, but after Mum died I was so scared Social Services would take him. I had been in care myself. I know what it's like to feel that you don't belong anywhere or with anyone, and I was prepared to do anything to keep Gino with me.'

'Including sacrificing your virginity,' Raul said harshly. 'Did you really think you could hide your innocence from me?'

Colour flared in Libby's pale face. 'I hadn't expected the experience to be so traumatic,' she admitted ruefully.

Guilt kicked Raul in his gut. 'It should not have been. If I'd had any idea that it was your first time I would have been more patient.' He had probably terrified the life out of her, he acknowledged, looking away from her as he recalled how his hunger for her had made him plunder her untutored body with a savagery that now filled him with shame.

'I assure you I will be much gentler next time,' he promised tautly.

Next time! Libby bit her lip. 'Does that mean you intend for our marriage to continue? Even though I…?' She stumbled to a halt, and Raul's dark brows lifted sardonically.

'Even though you deceived me and married me under false pretences?' he queried coolly. 'I admit my first thought was to send you back to England, but apart from the fact that Gino needs you, it is also possible that you have already conceived my child. I realise that when we made love it was not a great experience for you, but it certainly worked for me,' he said self-derisively. 'I did not use contraception, and it is perfectly feasible that you are pregnant.'

Libby's heart clenched at the idea that she might be carrying Raul's baby. She seemed to be on an emotional roller-coaster, and she hugged her arms around her body as a little tremor of excitement ran through her.

Raul frowned. 'You're cold. Let's go back to the house.'

He walked beside her along the jetty, but Libby was so intensely aware of him that she stumbled, and would have fallen into the water if it had not been for his lightning reactions. He caught hold of her shoulder to steady her, stared at her white face for a second, and then scooped her into his arms, ignoring her protest as he strode towards the house.

'You can barely stand. You're wasting your energy fighting me, *cara*, because I'm not going to let you go,' he warned her, and he knew as he said the words that he meant them. Somehow Libby had crept under his guard, and to his surprise he was in no hurry to evict her.

CHAPTER NINE

THE steady thud of Raul's heart beneath her ear soothed Libby's ragged emotions, and the strength of his arms holding her felt comfortingly safe. Wasn't that what she had longed for when she was a child? she thought ruefully. To feel safe and protected? She had never doubted that her mother had loved her, but she had disliked most of Liz's hippy boyfriends, and had yearned for the security of a proper home and a family. Had she been drawn to Raul from the moment she had met him because her instincts had told her that he was a strong and powerful man whom she could trust?

He strode through the house, and her heart skittered when, instead of heading for his study or the sitting room, he carried her up the wide staircase to the master bedroom.

'We need to talk,' he growled as he lowered her onto the bed.

To her consternation he sat down next to her—so close that she could feel the warmth of his body and breathe in the intoxicating scent of his cologne, mixed with another scent that was intensely male.

She twisted her fingers together in her lap and said quietly, 'I don't suppose you'll believe me, but I felt really guilty about lying to you. You have every right to be angry.'

She sounded so convincing that Raul found it impossible to believe she was a clever actress. And even if she was, what difference did it make? He had married her to gain control of Carducci Cosmetics, and his other reasons were still valid: Gino, the desire for a child of his own, and his overwhelming desire for her that still burned with a white-hot flame.

He reached out and idly wrapped a flame-coloured curl around his finger. 'I suppose I understand why you did it,' he said heavily, and realised that it was true. He was still angry with her for her deception, but he could not help feeling a begrudging admiration that she had fought so hard to keep Gino. 'If I had been in the same situation I too would have done anything to prevent Gino from being taken into care. The memories I have of living in the orphanage are not happy ones.'

'How old were you when you were adopted?'

'Seven.'

'I was that age when I was allowed to leave my foster home and live with Mum again. We went to Ibiza soon after. Do you know anything about your real parents?' Libby asked him curiously.

'Only that they lived in dire poverty in the backstreets of Naples. My mother died shortly after giving birth to me, and for the first few years of my life I lived with my father.' Raul grimaced. 'My memories of him are of a big, brutal man—and the feel of his belt across the backs of my legs. He was an alcoholic, although of course I did not understand that then. All I knew was that he had an unpredictable and violent temper. He died when I was five. I don't know what happened to him, although I suspect he was a member of a criminal gang. One night he went out, leaving me alone as he often did, and later police officers broke down the door of our flat and took me to an orphanage.

'I was a difficult child, and the nuns who ran the orphanage struggled to control me. No one wanted to foster me, and it seemed likely I would spend the rest of my childhood in care. But Pietro and Eleanora Carducci were prepared to give me a chance. I don't know why they chose to adopt a feral street boy,' Raul said, his hard features softening as he remembered his adoptive parents, 'but I am thankful that they did. My life changed for ever because of them, and I will be eternally grateful for all they did for me.'

Libby nodded, her heart aching as she imagined Raul as the brutalised and unhappy little boy he must have been before he had been adopted. 'Life can be so precarious,' she murmured, 'and children are so vulnerable. All I want is for Gino to grow up feeling safe and secure and confident that he is loved.'

'Together we will do everything possible to give him a happy childhood,' Raul assured her. 'But is that really all you want, Libby? Was Gino's welfare truly the only reason you married me?'

She tensed as he slid his hand beneath her chin and tilted her face. He had moved along the mattress and was now so close that she could see the tiny lines that fanned out around his eyes. Last night those eyes had glittered with icy fury, but now, incredibly, there was a warmth in his gaze that gave her hope. 'I didn't marry you for financial gain, I swear,' she said urgently. 'I don't want your money.'

His sensual smile stole her breath. 'Then what *do* you want, *cara*?'

The atmosphere shifted subtly, and Libby's heart-rate quickened when he brought his other hand up and smoothed her hair back from her face. Suddenly shy, she dropped her gaze, but staring at his lap made her heart beat faster still. She had a vivid recall of what was hidden beneath his trousers: long, muscular legs, and strong thighs covered with wiry dark hair that grew thicker at the base of his masculinity. Hot-cheeked, she dragged her gaze away from that pertinent area of his body. But she could not forget his promise that the next time they had sex he would be gentler, and as she lifted her eyes to his mouth she couldn't help wondering when that next time might be.

The stinging sensation when he had taken her virginity had caused her to cry out more from shock than actual pain, but now she was aware of a restless ache low in her pelvis that grew stronger when she remembered how he had caressed her with his wickedly inventive tongue.

'I regret that losing your virginity was not the special experience it should have been. But I think you found some aspects of lovemaking enjoyable—am I right, Libby?' he queried softly.

'I...' Libby was transfixed by the sultry heat in his eyes that made her skin prickle and her nipples tingle.

Raul did not love her, and had never given her any reason to hope that he ever would. But he wanted them to remain married, and that was better than nothing, she told herself. He was going to be a wonderful father for Gino, and for any children they might have. She gave a tiny shiver of excitement at the thought that she might already have conceived his baby. A marriage of convenience might not be perfect, but she was a realist and accepted that few things in life were. After all, she had never expected to have a husband and children after she had vowed to devote herself to Gino. Raul was an unexpected bonus, and as long as she kept the fact that she loved him to herself, their marriage stood every chance of being a success.

'You don't seem very sure,' he murmured, his deep, gravelly voice whispering across Libby's skin so that she gave another shiver. 'I think it's time I showed you how pleasurable sex can be.'

Libby swallowed, her heart thudding so hard beneath her ribs that she snatched a shallow breath. He mistook the sudden tension that gripped her, and ran his fingertips lightly up and down her spine, as if he were soothing a nervous colt.

'Don't be afraid, *cara*. I will be gentle this time.'

And as if to prove his words the first brush of his lips across hers was as soft as gossamer, a delicate tasting that was sweetly beguiling and instantly left her aching for more.

When he kissed her again she opened her mouth and kissed him back. He framed her face with his hands, grazing his lips over hers until she gave a frustrated moan and curled her arms around his neck in a clumsy attempt to make him kiss her with all the wild, pent-up passion she sensed he was trying to control.

Libby's eagerness was irresistible, but Raul also found it strangely touching now that he knew how inexperienced she was. When she dipped her tongue tentatively into his mouth he groaned, his restraint pushed to its limits, and without lifting his lips from hers he tumbled them both backwards, so that they were lying on the bed.

He could not rationalise what was happening to him, he acknowledged as he drew her jumper over her head, startled to find that his hands were shaking. He had been furious when he'd realised that it had not been necessary for him to marry her, but since then he had been coming up with reasons why she should remain his wife.

He was not prepared to let her go—at least not yet. Maybe not for a very long time… The fact that she had not been Pietro's mistress made him happier than it had any right to, because of course it was only desire that pumped through his veins, nothing more. He had fallen in lust the moment he had laid eyes on her, and now that she was his wife he could enjoy the single most important benefit of being married as far as he was concerned: regular sex with a woman who could decimate his self-control with a single look from her blue-green eyes.

He stared down at her pale, slender body. Her breasts were surprisingly full and rounded, her pink nipples already puckering, inviting him to close his mouth around them. She was watching him warily, and he knew he must control his impatience and indulge in leisurely foreplay until she was fully aroused and ready for him to possess her. He kissed her again—a long, slow tasting that left them both breathing hard—and then deftly removed her jeans.

He stood up to strip off his trousers, and saw the doubtful glance she cast at the solid length of his erection. 'Trust me, *cara*, it will be good for you this time,' he assured her, and he stretched out on the bed and claimed her mouth with hungry passion. Her unrestrained response stirred his soul, and his hand shook again as he cupped her breast and gently stroked his thumb pad over its dusky crest.

Heat unfurled in the pit of Libby's stomach when Raul lowered his head to her breast and flicked his tongue back and forth across her nipple until it felt tight and swollen. The sensation was exquisite, and she arched her back, a sigh of pleasure escaping her when he transferred his mouth to her other breast and meted out the same delicious torture. The restless longing he had evoked the first time he had made love to her returned, and was even fiercer in its intensity. The slight soreness between her legs had faded, and she ached for him to touch her there, but he continued to caress her breasts, now sucking hard on one nipple while he rolled its twin between his fingers until the pleasure was unbearable.

Only when she made a guttural plea did he trail his hand lightly over her stomach and thighs, and she caught her breath when at last he threaded his fingers through the cluster of tight curls and slowly, oh, so slowly parted her, stretching her with infinite care so that he could slide one digit fully into her. She lifted her hips as he withdrew his finger a little way and then pushed deeper, in and out, with pumping little movements that caused a curious fluttering sensation deep in her pelvis.

Something was happening to her that she had no control over—a wondrous coiling sensation that grew tighter and tighter as his hand moved rhythmically, caressing her with delicate little strokes so that molten heat flooded between her legs. Frantically she curled her fingers into the sheet and closed her eyes, so that she could focus on the tiny spasms that were now rippling across her belly. Her breathing quickened and became sharp little gasps as he took her higher and higher to some unknown place that she was desperate to reach, and she gave a sob of protest when he suddenly withdrew his finger, leaving her bereft and empty.

'Please...' She could barely articulate the word, her limbs trembling, needing him to touch her again and take her to the end of the journey he had started. She felt him move, and her lashes flew open to see him position himself over her. The feel of the solid length of his erection pushing against her thigh made her heart pound.

'Try to relax, *cara*,' he said deeply, his voice shaking with his desire to sink his throbbing shaft into her, but recognising the importance to take it slow so that he did not hurt her. 'You are ready for me,' he assured her, but still he hesitated and rubbed his finger against the moist, swollen lips of her vagina.

Libby gasped when he found the tiny, ultra-sensitive nub of her clitoris, and she jerked suddenly, her eyes widening with stunned disbelief as the coiling inside her snapped. The spasms grew stronger, making her muscles convulse in wave after wave of indescribable pleasure, but she soon realised that this was just the beginning, for Raul was easing forward, and she instinctively bent her knees to allow him to penetrate her with one slow, careful thrust, sliding deeper, inch by inch, until he filled her to the hilt.

'*Oh!*' The feel of him inside her was so incredible that she could not restrain a soft moan, but he stilled instantly and rested his sweat-beaded brow against hers, his eyes dark with regret.

'Does it hurt? I'll stop…'

'No!' She clutched his shoulders as he

withdrew a little, and urged him down so that he sank deeper once more. 'Don't stop.'

The first waves of pleasure were receding, but when he drew back again and then thrust forward, gentle at first, but then faster and harder, she sensed a new wave building, sweeping her inexorably higher and higher, so that she groaned and twisted her head on the pillows. Raul gripped her hips and held her while he continued to drive into her, each stroke more powerful and intense than the last. She was so nearly there. He paused, and she sobbed his name until he relented and stroked again, and then the world exploded in a series of exquisite spasms that racked her body so that she raked her nails down his back, utterly blown away by her first orgasm.

She knew from the harsh sound of his breathing that he was nearing his own nirvana, and her generous heart yearned for him to experience the same bliss that he had gifted her. Instinctively she lifted her legs higher and wrapped them around his hips, so that he could thrust deeper still. Now the feeling of him pumping inside her was even more intense, and impossible to withstand—for either of them. Raul threw his head back, his face a rigid mask as he teetered on the brink for as long as he could hold on to his self-control before it shattered spectacularly and he crashed over the edge, taking Libby with him and revelling in her cries of pleasure as she climaxed for a second time.

He had sensed that Libby was an intensely sensual and passionate woman, and now he had proof, Raul mused as he lay lax on top of her, utterly sated and so amazingly relaxed that he felt boneless and strangely complete—as if he had been waiting for this moment, with this woman, all his life. She had spoiled him for other women, and he almost resented the hold she had over him. The idea of having sex with anyone else was repugnant—and as for her ever giving her body to another man! Fire burned in his gut and a murderous black rage swept through him. He would tear the man apart with his bare hands. Libby was *his* woman, *his* wife, and he would never let her go.

Inferno! Where had that thought come from? he wondered impatiently. He had done the whole intense relationship thing once, and sworn that he would rather eat poison than repeat the miserable experience. Libby meant nothing to him. He viewed their marriage as a partnership based on their mutual desire to bring Gino up as part of a family—with astounding sex thrown in.

With that settled, Raul gently disengaged his body from Libby and saw that she had fallen asleep. She did not stir, simply snuggled up to him like a sleepy kitten, instinctively searching for warmth, her glorious hair spilling over the pillows and her long gold lashes fanning her velvet soft cheeks.

A partnership, he reminded himself firmly. Yes, she was very beautiful—even when she insisted on wearing all the colours of the rainbow at the same time. But he had learned that the best recipe for a successful marriage was one that did not include messy emotions, and he would *not* be moved by the flame-haired siren who was sleeping peacefully, with her head resting on his chest and her cheek pressed against his heart.

The sound of Gino's gurgling laughter roused Libby from a deep sleep. She stirred and stretched luxuriantly, wakefulness alerting her to the feeling of slight tenderness between her thighs. But that was only to be expected after Raul had made love to her so passionately in the early hours of the morning. She turned her head, and her heart flipped when he strolled in off the balcony, holding Gino in his arms.

Every time she looked at him she was struck anew by how gorgeous he was, and this morning, wearing a pair of close-fitting faded jeans and a black polo shirt, he stole her breath. He was laughing as Gino vigorously explored his ear with a chubby finger, and his tender expression as he smiled at the baby filled Libby with despair. How could she not love him? she thought helplessly. He was impossibly handsome, sinfully sexy, and heartbreakingly gentle with the little boy he intended to adopt as his son.

She quickly sat up, struggling to bring her emotions under control, and two pairs of dark eyes fringed with ridiculously long black lashes immediately turned to her.

'*Buongiorno, cara.*' Raul's grin revealed a set of very white teeth which looked even more blinding in contrast to his olive gold skin. A lock of hair had fallen onto his brow, and she remembered how she had threaded her fingers through its silky blackness and held his head to her breasts during their early-morning sex session.

She blushed at the sultry gleam in his eyes which told her that he was remembering it too. An elusive message passed between them that was gone before she could grasp it or understand it. But his gaze remained locked with hers, and her heart ached as it had done when he had made love to her a second time, with such surprising tenderness that afterwards tears had trickled from the corners of her eyes and he had gently kissed them away.

'Gino's had his breakfast and a bath, and I've taken him for a stroll around the garden,' Raul informed her. 'I think he'll be ready for a nap pretty soon.'

'It's nearly midday,' Libby murmured after a horrified glance at the clock. 'You should have woken me.'

'Silvana was happy to take charge of him. I think she expected you to be tired after your wedding night.'

'Oh, God!' Libby covered her scarlet cheeks with her hands. 'What must she think?'

'That you were worn out after a very energetic night with your new husband,' Raul said in a tone of extreme satisfaction. He sat on the edge of the bed and leaned forward to brush his mouth over hers in a lingering kiss that did not last nearly long enough. 'I'm sure she will understand that you may need to lie in and recuperate most mornings from now on.'

His grin was impossible to resist. Libby's lips twitched. 'You can take that insufferably smug smile off your face, *Signor* Carducci.'

'Make me, *Signora* Carducci,' he challenged softly.

He was prevented from kissing her again by Gino, who had grown bored with not being the centre of attention and now butted his head against Raul's shoulder. 'I'll take him to the nursery while you get up,' he said, getting to his feet and swinging Gino high in the air, much to the baby's delight. 'Silvana will mind him for a few hours. I thought you might like to come sailing with me.'

Libby threw him a startled glance. In the days leading up to their marriage he had spent many hours with her and Gino, but she had been under no illusion: the focus of his attention had been the baby. Her heart skipped at the idea that he wanted to be alone with her. She would fly to the moon with him if he asked, but she must not seem too eager or he might guess that her feelings for him were much more than lust and platonic friendship.

'Don't you have to work?' she queried.

True to his word, he had worked from his study rather than drive in to the Carducci Cosmetics offices in Rome each day, and on several occasions he had asked her to read through various documents and sign them. This had caused a certain amount of tension when she had questioned some of his proposals. Admittedly she hadn't really understood the finer details, but she could add up figures and was concerned by the level of risk in some of his ventures. To her surprise he hadn't argued with her, but simply filed the documents away, saying that perhaps she was right and he should be more cautious.

She hoped that her involvement in running CC would not create friction between them, she brooded. But all thoughts of the company, and indeed anything else, were wiped from her mind when his mouth curved into a sensual smile.

'Certainly not. This is our honeymoon, *cara*, and I think we should use the opportunity to get to know each other better. What do you think?'

I think I may have died and gone to heaven, Libby thought shakily. But somehow she managed a casual shrug. 'Sailing sounds good to me.'

It was beautiful out on the lake. The sun shone brilliantly in a cloudless sky, and a little breeze tugged the sails of Raul's boat and sent it skimming across the water. Libby sat with her arm propped on the boat rail and stared down at the crystal clear water.

'This is wonderful,' she murmured happily.

Raul was doing something with the sail. He had explained the technicalities of sailing to her, but she preferred to simply enjoy the scenery. The lake was a dense blue that reflected the sky, the green foliage of trees ringed the shore, and in the distance were the graceful turrets of the famous Odescalchi Castle.

'Have you never sailed before?' he asked her.

'I've never been on any sort of boat before—apart from a pedalo once. There's not much opportunity to mingle with the yachting fraternity at a South London comprehensive,' she said dryly. 'When did *you* learn to sail?'

'When I was a boy—Pietro taught me. I love the sense of freedom out here on the lake. It's where I come whenever I'm feeling tense.'

Libby digested this information and gave a faint frown. 'Does that mean you're feeling tense now?'

'Only certain areas of my anatomy, *cara*.' His eyes gleamed wickedly when Libby blushed, but she could not prevent herself from staring at the distinct bulge beneath his tight-fitting jeans.

'Oh!'

Raul was still grinning when he brought the boat up to a little wooden jetty which ran out from a secluded beach at the edge of the lake. An attractive summerhouse sat close to the water's edge, and tall pine trees provided shade and privacy.

'This land is all part of the Villa Giulietta's estate,' he explained to Libby. 'You can only reach the summerhouse by boat, and no one ever comes here but me.'

'A secret copse—how lovely,' she murmured, sternly telling herself that she must not read too much into the fact that he had brought her to his private hideaway. 'The trees shield the house so well that I doubt anyone sailing past would even know it's here.'

Her heart missed a beat when Raul came up behind her and slid his arms around her waist.

'Mmm… And as we are safe from prying eyes, there is no reason why I shouldn't do this,' he said softly, pushing her hair aside and trailing his lips up her neck before he nibbled her earlobe.

Tiny darts of pleasure shivered through

Libby, and she made no effort to resist him when he tugged the straps of her sundress over her shoulders so that her breasts spilled into his hands. The feel of his warm palms cradling her naked flesh was intoxicating, and she gasped when he rolled her nipples between his fingers until they swelled into stiff peaks. Molten heat flooded between her legs, her desire for him instant and over-whelming. But even so she could not help feeling stupidly shy when he pushed her dress down over her hips so that it pooled at her feet and she was left standing before him in just skimpy white lace knickers.

'Raul…?'

'No one can see us,' he assured her thickly. 'I need you now, *cara*.'

His eyes blazed into hers as he pulled her pants down and slipped his hand between her thighs, and there was tenderness in his smile when he discovered the slick wetness of her arousal. He lifted her and carried her over to a patch of soft grass in the cool shade of the trees, stripping out of his clothes with flattering haste and coming down beside her to claim her mouth in a hungry kiss that de-manded her eager response.

Fingers of sunlight filtered through the dense foliage of the trees and dappled their bodies. Libby could see tiny patches of blue sky between the green leaves, but as Raul lowered his head and suckled one taut nipple and then the other, she closed her eyes and gave herself up to the pleasure of his mouth. She bit her lip when he pushed her legs apart and flicked his tongue across her clitoris, back and forth, until she twisted her hips urgently, needing to feel him inside her. He was already massively aroused, but fascination made her bold, and she touched him, smiling at his swiftly indrawn breath when she closed her hand around the hard length of his erection and gently squeezed.

Raul withstood her ministrations for a few torturous minutes before he groaned and captured her hand, his breathing ragged as he fought to regain his self-control.

'Enough, witch…' he muttered hoarsely, and eased into her, pausing while her muscles stretched to accommodate him before he thrust deeper, again and again, in an age-old rhythm that quickly drove them to the edge. *'Tesoro…'*

The word was ripped from his throat as they climaxed simultaneously, Libby's vaginal muscles tightening and rippling around him, giving him the most intense pleasure he had ever experienced.

Afterwards, when they lay still joined, she wondered what the word meant, but she was afraid to ask in case she had imagined the closeness she sensed between them, the feeling that their souls as well as their bodies had merged.

CHAPTER TEN

AFTER that they went sailing regularly, and always stopped off at the hidden summerhouse. The glorious days of early summer slipped past, and before Libby knew it, it was June, and Gino's first birthday.

'I can't believe he's walking and saying a few words,' she said softly, when she and Raul tucked the worn out little boy into his cot that evening.

'He said Papa quite clearly when we lit the candle on his cake,' Raul said with undisguised pride in his voice. 'Did you hear him?'

Libby gave him a mock frown. 'I still think it sounded more like Mamma. Do you think he enjoyed his party?'

It had only been a small affair; the Vincentis had brought their two daughters, and several of Raul's other friends whom Libby had met at the dinner parties they had attended had also come with their children.

'One year old already,' she murmured, the familiar surge of love flooding through her when she stared down at Gino's flushed cheeks and silky black curls. 'I wish Mum could see him,' she whispered, tears filling her eyes.

Raul pulled her close. 'She would be very proud of you for being such a wonderful mother to him,' he assured her gently, conscious of the curious tugging on his heart that had caught him unawares so often recently. 'Don't cry, *cara*.' It tore him apart when she cried. 'Come with me. I've got something to show you.'

Puzzled, Libby allowed him to lead her out of the nursery and up several flights of stairs. 'We must be at the top of the tower,' she said breathlessly. 'Where are we going, Raul?'

'In here.' He pushed open a door and stood back for Libby to enter the room, grinning when her mouth opened in astonishment but no sound emerged. 'It's your art studio,' he explained unnecessarily as she stared around— at the large easel set close to a window which overlooked the lake, the stack of blank canvases, the shelves containing paints and other equipment. The paintings Libby had left behind in Cornwall were arranged around the room, and she felt a little swell of pride as she studied them. They really weren't bad, she decided.

'A friend of mine owns a gallery in Rome,' Raul told her as he joined her in front of a beach scene she had painted just before she had come to Italy. 'I showed him some of your work and he's very keen to organise an exhibition. What do you think of the studio?' he asked, concerned by her lack of response to something that he had taken great pleasure in organising for her. '*Cara*, why are you crying? If you don't like it…'

'I *do* like it—of course I do.' Libby sniffed inelegantly and gave him a blinding smile as she launched herself into his arms. 'It's the nicest, most wonderful thing anyone has ever done for me, and I love—' She stopped herself just in time and changed 'you' to 'it'. 'Oh, Raul, I don't know how to thank you.'

'I'll show you, *cara*,' he promised wolfishly. 'There is a very good reason why I had a sofa put up here—as I am about to demonstrate.'

Was it tempting fate to admit that she was the happiest she had ever been in her life? Libby mused a few weeks later, as she got

ready for a dinner party that she and Raul
were to attend that evening. Life couldn't be
more perfect. Gino was a gorgeous, energetic
little boy who was happiest toddling around
the gardens of the Villa Giulietta. Libby
adored being with him, but she appreciated
the couple of hours a day when Silvana took
charge of him, leaving her free to go up to
her studio and paint.

Raul continued to work from the villa, and
only drove in to his office in Rome when absolutely necessary. She loved the fact that she
could pop in to his study and see him whenever she could think of an excuse, and he
often invited her to join him to discuss plans
and proposals for Carducci Cosmetics.

But if the days were good, the nights were
heaven, she mused, smiling when she stared at
her flushed cheeks in the mirror and realised
that there was no need to apply blusher. Her
fears that the sizzling sexual chemistry between her and Raul would die out had proved
unfounded. They could not get enough of one
another, and their lovemaking was more passionate and intense than ever. She loved the
way he made love to her, Libby thought, feeling her breasts grow heavy at the memory of
how he had joined her in the bath the previous
night. It had taken ages to mop up the floor

after they had caused a small tidal wave with the bathwater, she recalled with a smile.

'Libby, we have to go.'

She turned as he entered the bedroom, and held her breath when he halted and studied her. 'I thought I'd tone down the colour scheme for once,' she said doubtfully when he seemed to be struck dumb. 'Do you think white is a bit, well…virginal?' When she'd tried the dress on she had thought that the simple white silk sheath overlaid with chiffon and decorated with tiny crystals on the bodice and narrow shoulder straps suited her, but now she wasn't so sure.

'It's rather too late for virginal, *cara*.' His eyes gleamed wickedly, but his voice was curiously rough as he said, 'You take my breath away.' He moved towards her and took something from his jacket pocket. 'My mother often wore this to parties,' he explained, and Libby gasped when he held up a necklace of shimmering diamonds that sparkled brilliantly in the light. 'The Carducci diamonds are a family heirloom.'

'I can't wear it,' Libby protested in a panicky voice. 'It must be worth a fortune. Suppose I lose it? Really,' she insisted, when he ignored her and fastened the necklace around her throat. 'I'm not a jewellery person.'

'I know,' Raul murmured dryly.

The only item of jewellery she wore was the plain gold band he had given her on their wedding day. On a recent trip to Rome he had taken her to an exclusive jewellers and tried to persuade her to choose a bracelet and perhaps matching earrings, but she had refused, saying that there was no point in her having expensive jewellery when she spent most of her time playing in the sandpit with Gino.

Libby was so different from his first wife— from any other woman he had ever met. And to think he had accused her of being a gold-digger. He shuddered at the memory of how he had treated her when she had first arrived at the villa. His divorce from Dana had left him deeply cynical about relationships, but Libby had changed his attitude, changed *him*, and he wondered what had happened to his much vaunted idea of an emotionless marriage.

'Wear the necklace tonight and allow me to show off my Carducci bride?' he requested softly.

And, as usual, Libby found that she could not refuse him.

* * *

'*Zia* Carmina is looking forward to seeing you tonight,' Raul told Libby as he swung the Lamborghini onto the driveway of his aunt's house in a fashionable suburb of Rome.

Privately, Libby doubted that. On the previous two occasions when they had visited his aunt, Carmina had been polite to her in front of Raul, but cold and unfriendly the moment he was out of earshot. He was fond of his mother's sister, she reminded herself. And for that reason she was determined to try and get on with Carmina.

Raul's aunt greeted him with a kiss on each cheek, but she stiffened when Libby stepped towards her and her smile slipped. 'I see you are wearing the Carducci diamonds,' she commented tightly.

'Yes…' Libby hesitated. 'Raul asked me to wear them.'

Carmina gave her a strange look. 'Did he, indeed?' she said softly, and something in her tone sent a shiver down Libby's spine.

Dinner was an ordeal. Carmina was a patron of numerous charities, and a well-known figure among Rome's social elite, and Libby was sure she had deliberately invited guests who were either brilliant academics or stunningly beautiful models to emphasise Libby's lack of education and social graces.

She felt hopelessly out of her depth as she struggled to join in the conversation around the table, and jealousy burned like corrosive acid in her stomach every time the gorgeous Italian television presenter sitting next to Raul leaned close to him and said something that made him laugh.

To her relief, coffee was served in the salon. She declined a cup when the waiter brought it round on a tray. For some reason she had gone right off coffee, the smell of it made her feel nauseous. Rather than watch Raul, who was still chatting to Miss Daytime TV, she wandered into the smaller sitting room next door to the salon—but immediately turned on her heel when she saw Carmina sitting on the sofa.

'I'm sorry... I—'

'Don't scurry away.' Raul's aunt gave her a cold smile, her eyes fixed on the necklace around Libby's throat. 'I wouldn't read too much into Raul giving you the diamonds,' she advised harshly. 'I had always hoped that one day *I* would wear the symbol of the Carducci bride,' she went on after a pause. 'After Eleanora died I thought that Pietro would turn to me. Not immediately, of course, but eventually. I loved him first, you see, before my sister had even met him. But when he saw Eleanora he chose her.'

'I'm sorry,' Libby said again, not knowing what else she could say.

'Pietro could have had me, but instead he chose a cheap little tart like you,' Carmina said bitterly.

'Actually, he didn't.'

Clearly Raul had not told his aunt that she was not Gino's mother, and that she hadn't been Pietro's mistress. Libby did not feel that she owed Carmina an explanation, but she'd had enough of the older woman's foul accusations. She opened her mouth to speak, but Carmina ignored her.

'And now you are a Carducci bride. I suppose you decided that losing control of your son's shares in Carducci Cosmetics was a small price to pay for becoming the wife of a billionaire?'

'Pardon?' Libby frowned as she tried to make sense of Carmina's statement. 'I don't know what you mean,' she mumbled, filled with a sudden sense of foreboding that made her heart thud painfully beneath her ribs.

There was a strangely triumphant expression in Carmina's eyes. 'Surely you read Pietro's will? It quite clearly states that if Gino's mother were to marry, his fifty percent share of CC would pass to Raul until the boy reaches adulthood. I had forgotten about the clause until I came across a copy of the will a few days ago, when I was tidying my bureau, and then everything made sense. Raul married you to claim full control of the company.'

The room swayed alarmingly, and Libby's legs suddenly seemed incapable of holding her. She sank down onto a chair. 'I did read the will,' she said shakily. But not properly, she thought, feeling sick, remembering how she been holding Gino when Raul had handed her the legal document. She had quickly skimmed down the first page and read the bit about Gino and his mother being able to live at the Villa Giulietta, but Gino had been squirming in her arms and she had handed the papers back because she'd been worried that the baby might tear them. It had all been so astounding and unexpected, and before she'd had time to blink Raul had whisked her off to Italy and she hadn't given the will another thought.

'Perhaps you would like to refresh your memory?' Carmina said softly. 'I was also a beneficiary of Pietro's estate—he bequeathed me some small items of jewellery—and I have a copy of the will here.' She crossed to the bureau, took some papers from the drawer, and dropped them in Libby's lap. 'The clause at the bottom of the second page is the one you should be interested in.'

Afterwards, Libby did not know how she managed to keep herself together for the remainder of the evening. Raul found her on the terrace, took one look at her white face and demanded to know what was wrong with her. She mumbled that she had a headache, hating him for playing the role of concerned husband when she knew it was just an act. At the beginning of the evening she would have been fooled by the compassion in his dark eyes, but now she knew what a snake in the grass he was. He had married her to get control of Carducci Cosmetics. The words of the clause in Pietro's will swirled round and round in her head, and she could not stifle a little moan of pain.

'*Dio!* Why didn't you tell me your headache was so bad?' he demanded roughly.

'I didn't like to interrupt you when you were having so much fun with the queen of the chat show,' Libby snapped.

'Gianna Mancini's son was a year old last week, and we were swapping baby development news,' he said with a wry smile. 'Her husband is away on business.' He paused, and then added quietly, 'You must know I only have eyes for you, *piccola*.'

Her heart yearned for the tenderness in his voice to be real, but she knew his performance was worthy of an Oscar. She dared not meet his gaze, terrified that he would see the devastation in hers, and to her relief he left her to collect her shawl while he went to bid farewell to his aunt, then hurried her out to the car.

On the journey home she closed her eyes, to convince him that her headache was too severe for her to be able to talk. He could not know that it was not her head but her heart that felt as though it had been ripped open, leaving a raw, agonising wound that she feared was irreparable.

'I'm going to check on Gino,' she muttered when they entered the villa, and hurried up the stairs before he had time to reply.

The baby was sleeping peacefully, his arms outstretched and the covers strewn about the cot as usual, where he had flung them off. Her desire to give Gino a father was the reason she had married Raul, she reminded herself—and knew she was lying. For her it had been love at first sight. She had fallen for Raul from the moment he had stormed into her life, had been drawn to him by a force beyond her control.

Gino loved him too, she acknowledged, tears slipping silently down her face when she pictured how the baby's face lit up whenever he saw Raul. Gullible fool that she was, she had swallowed Raul's story that he wanted to adopt Pietro's son and be a devoted father to him, but now she wondered if Raul had lavished attention on Gino as part of his cold-hearted plan to persuade her to marry him and thereby gain full control of the company.

Numb with misery, she crept out of the nursery. Instead of walking down the corridor to the master bedroom she turned and ran up the stairs leading to the tower. Tears were streaming down her face. She hadn't cried like this since her mother's funeral— great, tearing sobs that racked her frame and made her chest burn. She couldn't face Raul tonight, she thought despairingly. If he realised how much his deception had hurt her, he would also realise that she was in love with him.

But it was likely that when she didn't come to bed he would search for her. She took a ragged breath and glanced wildly around the studio. There was no lock on the door, but maybe she could drag the cupboard across it to prevent him from entering…

'Here you are. I thought you were going to bed?'

She jerked her head around at the sound of his voice, and her treacherous heart performed its usual somersault at the sight of him lounging in the doorway. His jacket was unfastened, as were the top few buttons of his shirt, revealing several inches of tanned skin and silky dark chest hair. He was so beautiful it was hardly surprising she had lost her heart to him. But he didn't want her heart—he never had—and to be fair he had not tricked her into marrying him by pretending to love her. It was her own fault that she had hoped and prayed and looked for any tiny sign that she meant something to him. When he had created the studio for her she had thought he had done it because he cared about her, but now she wondered if he had hoped she would become so absorbed in her artwork that she would not realise she was no longer involved in running CC.

Pain ripped through her; and with it a burning, blazing, incandescent rage that she had been so stupid, and he was such a deceitful, lying—

'Have you taken some painkillers for your

headache?' He took a step towards her, frowning when he saw that she had been crying. *'Cara...?'*

'Don't!' She put up a hand to ward him off. 'Don't *cara* me. Don't sound concerned when you couldn't give a damn.'

The tight band around her self-control snapped, unleashing her fiery temper, and driven by hurt and despair she snatched up the tub of orange paint she had blended from powdered pigment earlier that day and hurled it across the room. It hit him squarely on his chest, and he was instantly covered in liquid paint from shoulder to hip, while great splodges spattered both his legs.

For a few simmering seconds he stared at her in utter astonishment before he found his voice. *'Madre di Dio!* What's the matter with you? You crazy firebrand—have you gone mad?'

'On the contrary, I've finally come to my senses and seen what a sly, conniving, treacherous bastard you are.' Libby flung the words at him with the same force with which she had thrown the paint. 'Your aunt showed me the clause in Pietro's will—the clause on the second page that I didn't have time to read when you turned up in Pennmar and bullied me into agreeing to bring Gino to Italy.'

'I did not bully you.' Raul paused as the implication of her words sank in. He had completely forgotten that his aunt had a copy of the will. 'Why on earth did Carmina show you the will?'

'Because she hates me,' Libby told him flatly. 'She was in love with Pietro, and she still believes that I was his mistress. She must have guessed I didn't know about the clause stating that control of Gino's shares would pass to you if I were to marry.'

Panic churned inside her as she realised that Raul's aunt must have also guessed that she was in love with him. If she was that transparent, could Raul have guessed too? she wondered, feeling sick with humiliation.

She stared at him, and her heart splintered when she noted the faintly uncomfortable expression in his eyes. 'Can you deny that the reason you asked me to marry you was so that you would be able to claim full control of CC?'

'I don't deny that that was one of the reasons,' he said quietly. He gave a harsh laugh when she paled. 'What did you think, Libby? That I had fallen in love with you?'

'*No!* Of course not,' she denied instantly, colour storming into her cheeks. 'But I thought you loved Gino. You told me you wanted to adopt him.'

'Both those things are true.'

'Are they?' Now it was her turn give a mocking laugh. 'Maybe you just pretended to care for him because you knew how much I wanted him to grow up in a family and have a father, as I longed for when I was a child?' Her temper soared once more. 'I know I was wrong to pretend that I was Gino's mother, and I believe that I deserved your anger when you discovered the truth. But all the time you were furious with me for deceiving you, you knew—*you knew*.' Her voice rose shrilly. 'You were guilty of a far more cruel deception. You cold-bloodedly used my love for Gino to steal his shares.'

'I have not stolen his shares,' Raul said sharply. 'I admit I wanted full control of CC until Gino was eighteen, but only so that I could take the company forward and ensure that there *is* a company for him to inherit in the future.' He sighed. 'I don't wish to be disloyal about my father but he had allowed the company to stagnate. I knew we were in danger of losing our position as a world leader in the cosmetics market if we did not expand our product range and diversify into new areas of growth such as the perfume range we're about to launch, and I believed I needed to have full control of CC to implement my plans.

'*Dio*, Libby,' he growled savagely when she said nothing, just looked at him with angry accusation in her eyes. 'Can you blame me for wanting to protect the interests of the company I had expected to inherit? I was shocked beyond words when I learned that I would have to discuss every business plan with a woman who at that time I believed was my father's lap-dancer mistress. You were prepared to do anything to keep Gino, including deliberately fooling me into believing you were his mother. By the same token, when I realised you had not read that clause in Pietro's will, I seized the opportunity to claim Gino's shares.'

He paused, and felt as though his heart was being squeezed in a vice when he saw the shimmer of tears in her eyes. 'Like I said, gaining control of the company was *not* the only reason I married you. Gino was certainly an important factor—I love him as much as if he was my own child, and my greatest wish is to adopt him.'

'So you say,' Libby muttered scathingly. 'How can I ever believe you or trust you now?' She jerked backwards when he took a step towards her, closing her eyes in despair when the familiar musky scent of his cologne drifted around her. 'Stay where you are. I can't bear to be near you.'

Raul's jaw tightened. 'We both know that's not true. The sexual attraction between us was white-hot from the start. We've never been able to keep our hands off each other. Even when I thought I had good reason to despise you, I wanted you with a hunger I have never felt for any other woman. The prospect of having you share my bed every night was another very good reason for marrying you.'

He had married her for sex. Well, she'd known that, Libby reminded herself. So why did hearing him say it feel as if he had stabbed her through the heart? She stared at him wordlessly when he shrugged out of his paint-spattered jacket and dropped it on the floor, panic coiling inside her as he began to undo his shirt buttons.

'What are you doing?' she demanded shakily. Was he intending to prove that the sexual alchemy between them was as fierce as ever? However much she told herself that she hated him, her traitorous body was pathetically weak, and she was terrified she would be unable to resist him. 'As far as I'm concerned our marriage is over,' she flung at him bitterly. 'I won't be sharing your bed this night or any other.'

His trousers hit the floor, and she moved her eyes helplessly over his broad, muscular chest, covered in a mass of dark hair that arrowed down over his abdomen and disappeared below the waistband of his boxers.

His eyes narrowed on her flushed face. 'I could very easily make you eat your words, *cara*,' he drawled, but then to her surprise—and, although she despised herself for admitting it, her disappointment—he turned back to the door.

'Where...where are you going?'

'To have a shower. I can't walk through the house dripping paint everywhere. We will finish this conversation downstairs in ten minutes. Don't make me have to come and get you, Libby,' he warned her in a deceptively soft tone that made her realise his anger was tightly controlled.

What reason did he have to be angry? she brooded bitterly when she made her way slowly down the tower staircase a few minutes after him. He was the one who had deceived her; he was the one who had broken her heart. But of course he did not know that, and somehow she must hide her hurt from him.

To her relief the bedroom was empty, but the sight of the huge bed where he had made love to her so passionately, and lately with such tenderness, brought more tears to her eyes. How could she remain married to him, loving him as she did, but knowing that she would never be anything more to him than a convenient sex partner?

She could not sleep in here tonight. She dared not face him again until she had regained some semblance of control over her emotions. Brushing her hand impatiently over her wet face, she spun round—but before she could reach the door Raul appeared, his dark hair still damp from his shower, his black robe belted loosely around him.

'I'm going to sleep in one of the other bedrooms,' she said stiffly, and then gave a startled gasp when he scooped her into his arms and strode towards the bed. 'Put me down, Raul. Let me go.' It was a cry from the heart, and the wobble in her voice tore at his insides.

'I can't, *piccola*.' His refusal was heartbreakingly gentle, and her tenuous hold on her emotions cracked.

'You have to,' she wept, burying her face in her hands and rocking back and forth on the edge of the bed. 'I can't bear to be your wife any longer.'

Raul felt as though he had been kicked in the gut. Witnessing Libby's distress was sheer torture, but he knew that if he followed his instinct to haul her into his arms and kiss away her tears she would fight him like a wildcat.

'Listen to me,' he said urgently, hunkering down beside her. 'I need you to read something, and then, if you still feel the same way, I will—' He broke off, feeling as though an arrow had pierced his heart as he contemplated the utter bleakness of his life without her. 'I don't know what I will do, *cara mia*,' he admitted roughly.

Libby stared blindly at the document he had placed in her lap. 'I don't want to read it. I'll probably miss something important anyway—I'm good at that,' she said bitterly. 'You read it to me.'

'You don't trust me,' he said regretfully. 'I need you to see it with your own eyes.'

He moved to stand by the balcony window, staring out at the moonlight dancing across the lake, his heart slamming in his chest. Libby picked up the document and forced herself to concentrate on the few brief paragraphs.

'I don't understand,' she mumbled, after

reading the page three times. 'It says that even though I am married you are returning control of Gino's shares in Carducci Cosmetics to me until he is eighteen.' She shook her head. 'If you went to all the trouble of marrying me so that you could claim full control of CC, why have you returned half the control back to me? It doesn't make sense.'

'Doesn't it, *cara*?' Raul's voice sounded curiously constricted. 'Can you really think of no reason why I might have revoked that damn clause? Look at the date at the top of the page.'

Libby stared at it uncomprehendingly. 'But that was two weeks after our wedding.' She stood up, her eyes locked on Raul's hard profile, and she suddenly had the strangest feeling that he was deliberately avoiding meeting her gaze. 'Why did you do it, Raul?' she whispered. 'You had full control of CC—the thing you wanted most in the world—so why give it up?'

'Because I discovered that I wanted something infinitely more precious than control of the company.' At last he turned to face her, and Libby caught her breath at the raw emotion blazing in his eyes. 'I discovered that I wanted you to love me—as I love you, *tesoro*.'

Silence stretched between them, simmering with tension. At last Libby shook her head. 'You don't.' There was no quaver of doubt in her voice. She could not allow herself to be swayed by the tenderness in his rueful smile, or the fierce urgency in his eyes as he strode towards her and caught hold of her hands. 'You said love is an illusion, and that you would never fall in love after your bitter divorce from your first wife. You married me to claim control of CC—and maybe because you do really care for Gino,' she acknowledged slowly.

'I swear that I love him, *cara*, and I will care for him and protect him as his father— *my* father—would have done. You stole my heart from the first, Libby,' he said roughly, his voice shaking with emotion. 'I was drawn to you from the moment I laid eyes on you, but I hated myself for wanting my father's mistress. Marriage seemed the ideal solution—it would give me control of the company and you in my bed—but even before our wedding day I knew it was more than that. You fill my world with colour and laughter and a joy that I had not known it was possible to feel. My life will be a grey and lonely place if you leave me.'

Could it be true? Could she believe him?

Libby's heart was pounding so hard that it hurt to breathe and her hand trembled as she reached up and touched his damp eyelashes. 'Raul...?'

'I was planning to tell you about the clause in the will, and that I had reversed it,' he admitted gruffly. His throat ached, and it was hard to get the words out. 'I want us to make decisions about CC together, and build a successful company for Gino. But every day I kept putting it off. I was afraid you would realise I had fallen in love with you once you learned that I had returned Gino's shares to you, and I was scared you didn't feel the same way.'

'You? Scared?' Libby shook her head wonderingly, hope and a tremulous joy unfurling inside her when he lifted her hand to his mouth and pressed his lips against her knuckles.

'Oh, yes, *cara*. Scared stiff—because I knew that the only reason you had married me was to give Gino a father.'

Was this what sky divers felt as they were about to launch themselves out of a plane? Fear, excitement, and above all a desperate hope? Was she imagining the love blazing in Raul's eyes?

'Gino wasn't the only reason,' she admitted

huskily. 'I love you, Raul. I can't remember a time when I didn't. Everything before I met you seems distant and colourless. I missed Mum so much…' she swallowed hard '…but you made me feel alive again—even when you made me angry, and especially when you made love to me.' Her voice cracked and the tears she had been trying so hard to hold back slipped down her face. 'I never thought I could be this happy.'

'*Tesoro*. Don't cry. *Ti amo*.'

The words were wrenched from his soul. Love—something he had never expected to feel for any woman until Libby had turned his world upside down. He drew her against him, his whole body shaking as he claimed her mouth almost tentatively; a tidal wave of emotion stormed through him when he felt her sweet response.

'You stole my heart, *cara*.' The words were muffled against her throat as he kissed her feverishly—her hair, her brow, the tip of her nose—and tasted the salt of her tears when he pressed his lips to her eyelids. 'Will you stay with me, my golden girl, the love of my life, my wife?'

'Just try to send me away,' Libby said softly. 'Oh, Raul, I love you so much.'

'And I love *you*—madly, my crazy little

firecracker. You owe me a new suit, by the way,' he said, grinning when she blushed scarlet.

'I'm sorry,' she mumbled, thinking of his paint-spattered suit. 'I don't know what came over me.'

'I love your unpredictability, and your fiery temper, and your generous heart, *cara mia*. You and Gino are my world, and I could not ask for anything more than for the three of us to be a family.'

Her beautiful smile stole his breath. 'There's a chance that three will be four before too long. I don't know definitely yet, but I'm two weeks late,' she admitted softly.

'*Cara...*' Raul's throat worked convulsively as emotion overwhelmed him. For a moment he could not speak to tell her how much she meant to him, but when he claimed her mouth in a tender kiss he discovered that there was no need for words...

EPILOGUE

THE private art gallery was packed, the rooms buzzing with conversation as people crowded in front of the bold, brilliantly coloured paintings on display.

'Elizabeth Carducci is certainly a gifted artist,' an art critic from a national newspaper commented to the tall, handsome man who was standing at the back of the room. 'This exhibition is one of the most exciting I've ever attended. And of course the Galleria Farnese is one of the most prestigious contemporary galleries in Rome. There are several top collectors here`, and I've no doubt that Signora Carducci's work will soon be attracting international acclaim.'

'I am sure you are right,' the tall man murmured. 'And it is acclaim that is well deserved.'

The art critic glanced around the gallery. 'I've never met Signora Carducci, but I've heard that she is exceptionally beautiful. Can you point her out to me?'

'My wife is over there,' Raul replied, in a tone that caused the art critic to give him a nervous smile. 'In the green-and-orange dress,' he added dryly. 'As you can see, she is indeed beautiful.'

'What did you say to Carlo Vitenze that made him shoot off like a frightened rabbit?' Libby asked her husband when he strolled over to join her. 'He's a respected critic. I hope you haven't upset him.'

'I merely let him know that your husband is very possessive,' Raul said lightly. 'He seemed to get the message.' He dropped a kiss on his wife's soft mouth, his eyes gleaming when she immediately parted her lips. 'It doesn't surprise me that every man in this room cannot take his eyes off you. I can see I am going to have to lock you away in the highest tower of the Villa Giulietta.'

Libby gave him an impish smile. 'I already have two very special men in my life—and they are so incredibly handsome why would I be interested in anyone else? Careful, Gino,' she said gently as the energetic toddler rushed up to her. 'Mind the pram; your sister is asleep.'

'See Lissa,' Gino demanded.

Raul lifted him up so that he could look into the pram where three-month-old Elisabetta Rose was sleeping peacefully. 'There she is. You can give her a kiss when she wakes up,' he told the little boy.

His eyes met Libby's and his heart turned over when he saw the love that blazed in those blue-green depths. A love for him and their children which he returned a thousandfold.

'There are two very special ladies in my life—and they are so beautiful that they have captured my heart for all eternity,' he said softly. 'I love you, Libby.'

Three simple words that meant everything to her, Libby thought, blinking back the tears that filled her eyes.

Raul frowned in concern. 'Why are you crying, *cara*? The exhibition is wonderful.'

'Everything is wonderful,' she reassured him, wrapping her arms around his waist and smiling mistily up at him. 'I'm crying because I am the happiest woman in the world. You make me happy, Raul, you and Gino and Lissa, and I love you with all my heart.'